# PAUPER, BRAWLER AND SLANDERER

**ff**

# AMOS TUTUOLA

## Pauper, Brawler and Slanderer

*faber and faber*
LONDON · BOSTON

First published in 1987 by
Faber and Faber Limited
3 Queen Square London WC1N 3AU

Filmset by Wilmaset Birkenhead Wirral
Printed in Great Britain by
Richard Clay Ltd Bungay Suffolk
All rights reserved

*British Library Cataloguing in Publication Data*

Tutuola, Amos
Pauper, brawler and slanderer.
I. Title
823[F]   PR 9387.9.T8
ISBN 0–571–14714–3 (cased)
ISBN 0–571–14765–8 (pbk)

# AUTHOR'S NOTE
## THE YORUBA EXPRESSIONS

The Yoruba expressions which are used in most parts of this story cannot be compared with those of the English language. This is because some of the English expressions do not at times carry enough weight nor give the actual picture or intention intended. It is hoped, apart from clarity of expression, to introduce the key Yoruba words and expressions to non-Yorubas.

Some of the expressions used are:

*Ha! Ho! He!*: an expression of shock, surprise, etc. but fairly mild.

*Haa! Hoo! Hee!*: also an expression of shock, surprise, etc. but carrying more weight.

*Haaa! Hooo! Heee!*: means the same but carries much more weight.

*Huu! Huu-u!*: expression of wailing or as when somebody is lamenting over a loss, disappointment, death, etc.

At the same time the expressions of *Ha! Haa! Haa! Ho! Hoo! Hoo!* are of shock, lamentation, sadness, sorrow, pain, suffering, etc.

*Hun-un!* carries more weight than Hmm!

*Paga!* carries more weight than Alas! – a sudden despair, etc.

*Şio!* means 'nonsense' or to discredit somebody or something with disdain.

*Ho-o-o ro-o-o!* is an expression of great sudden despair and shock.

*Ye-e-e! (yay-ay-ay)* is a cry of severe pain, to lament, to think of an absent one with longing. *O!* to remember a forgotten thing, etc.

Furthermore, the following Yoruba titles are used in this story as well:

| YORUBA | ENGLISH |
|---|---|
| Ọba | King |
| Olori | Queen or queens |
| Kabiyesi | Your Worship or Your Majesty |
| Aafin | Palace |
| Ikọ | Messenger, envoy, deputation, etc. |
| Baalẹ | Governor, chief of a town or village |
| Ifa | The god of divination |

| Ọpẹlẹ | The Ifa's messenger or Ikọ through which the Ifa speaks to the Babalawo, the Ifa priest |
| Ọtun | Lieutenant, one holding place next in rank to the Ọba |
| Osi | The third rank to the Ọba but under the Ọtun – he is an internal auditor. He delivers everything he collects from people to the Ọtun who will then give all to the Ọba |

TO EXPLAIN THE 'ẸSẸNT'AYE' IN BRIEF

Before Babalawo starts to cast the Ọpẹlẹ upon the Irosu powder which is already spread inside the Ifa bowl, first of all he will take the baby from its father, he will press the sole of the baby's left foot upon the powder until the baby's foot-mark is well printed on it. After this, he will return the baby to its father. So this foot-mark is called 'Ẹsẹnt'aye' and it is at this time that the baby has become a real inhabitant of this earth.

But then the Babalawo will cast the Ọpẹlẹ upon the powder inside the Ifa bowl several times in order to get the correct 'odu', the indication of divination, and having got the kind of 'odu' with which the baby has come to the earth, then he will interpret it carefully to the father and the rest of the people who are present.

ẸSẸ  –  NTẸ  –  AYE
foot  contacts  earth

This is the meaning of this important word.

Amos Tutuola
Ibadan

# CONTENTS

# THE PRIMITIVE CUSTOM OF LAKETU TOWN

Two thousand years were past and had gone. There was a town which was at that time under a state called in the present century OGUN STATE, in the west of Nigeria. The name of that defunct town was called LAKETU.

In those days, Laketu town was indeed big and it was so populous that it was impossible to know the exact number of people who lived there.

The Ọba or King who reigned in that town in that century was very kind. He was indeed active and painstaking in everything which he did. He ruled his people with great patience because he loved them heartily. And in return, his deputy, chiefs and the people of the town loved him as well as they loved gold and silver. The Ọba also loved all those sojourners who lived in his land as he loved himself.

Farming was the main work which most people of this Ọba were doing. For this, abundant and surplus foodstuffs of different kinds were in the town always. But so many of those people were craftsmen such as the blacksmiths, carvers of the wooden bowls, all sorts of domestic utensils, well-diggers, fashion-makers, carvers of different kinds of images, makers of ornaments on the walls and pillars of the Ọba's Aafin or palace and on the walls and pillars of the chiefs' Aafin. And so many were hunters of big animals.

In this Laketu town, there was a strange rock on the outskirts of the town. This rock was exceedingly high. The circular bottom of it was more than one thousand kilometres. At the foot of this hideous rock, there was a very huge hole which went deeply into it.

So also, there was a pond of antiquity at the foot of the strange rock. It was very close to the huge hole. The sort of the water in this pond was so horrible as well that it used to scare the people of the town.

A very fearful voice which used to shake heavily both forest and wilderness around there and which terrified people used to come to the outside from the innermost of the huge hole. So this horrible voice caused the children, young and old people, to believe strongly that the huge hole truly went into the residence of Creator who was creating the people who were coming to the earth.

But as the Ọba, his chiefs and the people of the town believed strongly that the hole went into the residence of Creator, for this, the Ọba and his chiefs used to give very rich sacrifices to the horrible voice every year.

But as the custom of this Laketu town was, if a person committed a serious offence, if the offence deserved that there was no alternative than to expel him from the town, then the Ọba and his chiefs would take the offender to the strange rock. After the Ọba had cursed upon him in the name of Creator, the Ọba would fill to the brim a container with the strange water of the pond of antiquity and then he would pour it onto the offender.

Having done so, the Ọba's state Ikọ or messengers would drive him away from the town immediately.

But why was the offender driven away from the town immediately the forbidden water was poured on him? The reason is that the Ọba, his chiefs and the people of the town believed that if the offender still remained in the town till the forbidden water was dried on his body, epidemic disease such as influenza would besiege the town that year and by that a large number of people would die.

But according to the custom of Laketu town, when a baby was born, on the third day that it was born, its father would consult the Babalawo, the Ifa priest, to find out from the Ifa the kind of destiny which his new baby had chosen from Creator before leaving for earth. Finding how the life or future of a newborn baby will be on earth is called 'ẹsẹnt'aye'.

2

In fact, Creator blessed the Ọba of Laketu town with many children, sons and daughters. On Ọjọru (The Day of Confusion – Wednesday), one of Ọba's Olori or queens, gave birth to a beautiful male boy.

But according to the primitive custom of Laketu town, in the morning of the third day that the baby was born, the Ọba consulted the Babalawo, the Ifa priest, in his royal chamber. When he put his baby on his lap, he told the Babalawo to find out from the Ifa through Ifa's Iko, Ọpẹlẹ, how the 'ẹsẹnt'aye' or the future of his baby would be on earth.

Whether his baby would be rich or poor; good or bad; hard-working man or slothful; or whether it would taint the royal family: all these the Ọba just wanted to know from the Ifa.

Having cast his Ọpẹlẹ, the Ifa's messenger, on the floor several times, the Babalawo interpreted the 'ẹsẹnt'aye' of the baby to the Ọba very, very carefully, he said: 'Kabiyesi (Your Worship), the ruler of earth and second to gods!' The Babalawo bowed low for the Ọba and then he continued, he said: 'Truly, when this your baby is grown to his manhood!' The Babalawo went on as he pointed his right finger to the baby, he said: 'He will be as powerful as a giant and he will use the power on the farm more than all the rest of the farmers!'

The Babalawo bowed low and then he went further in his predictions to the Ọba. He said: 'Kabiyesi, but the harder this your baby works the more his poverty and wretchedness will become worse!'

But when the Ọba began to look dejected now, the Babalawo pointed his left finger to the Ọpẹlẹ (the Ifa's messenger or Iko) and his right finger to the baby. He continued his predictions: 'Kabiyesi, in the long run, you will drive this your baby away from your Aafin, when his poverty and wretchedness come to climax. Even after you have driven him away, it will not be so long before you will expel him away from the town!'

Having heard this again from the Babalawo, the Ọba was more shocked. In great grief and depression, he readjusted himself in his royal seat while his baby was still on his lap.

But then the Babalawo predicted further, he said: 'Kabiyesi, but

3

after your baby is banished from the town, and in his wandering on his endless journey, he will wander to a faraway town and the people of that town will install him as their Ọba!'

'Kabiyesi,' the Babalawo disclosed further, as the Ọba was then overwhelmed with sadness and was entirely drenched in his perspiration, 'in fact, this your baby will become an Ọba in a foreign town and there is nothing which can prevent him from being an Ọba. But it is a pity indeed that the destiny of poverty and wretchedness which he had chosen from Creator, will not let him keep long on the throne!'

The Babalawo advanced in his predictions to the Ọba, he said: 'The Ifa says but after this your baby is expelled from the throne, as it is the going of the water-flies which the people see and not their return, Kabiyesi, it is just so you will see only the "going" of this your baby but you will not see his "return" for ever! Although you and the other people will not see him for ever, he will still roam about on earth invisibly!

'Kabiyesi! The ruler of earth and second to gods! It is so the life (ẹsẹnt'aye) of your baby will be on earth when he grows to manhood! Let the crown keep long on your head and let the shoes keep long on your feet!' Thus the Babalawo concluded the predictions of the Ọba's baby that morning.

'But what kind of the sacrifice should I give to the Ifa in order to avert these bad omens on my lovely baby?' the Ọba asked greedily from the Babalawo.

'Haa, there is not any sacrifice which can appease the Ifa to avert these bad omens from your baby. Because he is really destined for all those things which will definitely happen to him in his manhood!' the Babalawo, Ifa priest, confirmed reluctantly to the Ọba.

But the Ọba was still sitting in his royal seat, greatly depressed, and his unfortunate baby was still on his lap, when the Babalawo packed his Ọpẹlẹ or the Ifa's Ikọ (messenger) back into his Ọpẹlẹ-bag and then he went back to his house that morning.

It was just 'the great grief which droops the head of an elder', for the Ọba that morning. He drooped his head heavily in great grief and he was unconscious. Great depression overwhelmed him so much that his mouth rejected food and drink.

4

However, when the baby was eight days old, he reluctantly gave him a name, which was Adegun.

In fact, as the Babalawo, the Ifa priest, had foretold the life of Adegun when he grew to the state of manhood, it was so his poverty and wretchedness became worse. The year that he farmed nearly without an end, it was that very year the swarm of the locusts used to come and invade his farm. They would eat the whole of his crops. The year that there were no locusts, there would not be sufficient rains for the crops to yield well. Thus the hard work which Adegun, the prince, was doing on his farm used to come to vanity every year.

Even if Adegun was a prince, he was wearing dirty rags about every day, as his poverty and wretchedness were so powerful. Whenever some persons pitied him for his miserable condition, and offered him some dresses, before daybreak, the termites would eat all into the rags on the racks on which he hung them.

But as it was a great grief to the Ọba to see one among his princes whose destiny was that of poverty and wretchedness, hereby, he began to hate Adegun. He did not like to see him any time at all. Because 'if a man's masquerade dances well; his dance will encourage him'. Adegun was not the sort of a good prince who he was supposed to be by the Ọba, chiefs and the people of the town as a whole. His unfortunate destiny discouraged them entirely.

## 2

## THE ỌBA EXPELS HIS PRINCE, ADEGUN,
## AWAY FROM HIS AAFIN

When the Ọba saw that as his prince was growing on so his poverty and wretchedness were becoming worse, then one morning, he invited into his royal chamber, his Deputy, Ọtun who was the father of the brawling lady. After, he sent for Osi, who was third in rank to him, and whose name was Kimi Adugbo, and who was the father of Alagẹmọ.

As soon as both of them arrived, in great passion and sadness, the Ọba told these his two high rank chiefs, how one of his princes chose but poverty and wretchedness from Creator instead of good fortunes.

But then in the presence of his Ọtun and Osi, and in great anger, he drove this his miserable prince out of his Aafin or palace. Because he as a prince was putting shame to the royal family. Although he was stronger even than a buffalo, poverty and wretchedness did not let him be a better young man in life like the other young farmers.

That was how a half of all the Babalawo's predictions years ago came to pass on Adegun, the wretched prince.

But it was in great sadness that both Deputy Ọba and Osi Ọba, Kimi Adugbo (stronghold of the neighbourhood) returned to their houses that morning. Their sadness was not because the Ọba drove his wretched prince away from his Aafin but because they too had the same problem with their own son and daughter as the Ọba had with his own prince.

It was not so long before Ọtun, the Ọba's Deputy, returned to his house in great grief and dejection. His breakfast was brought to him. But 'the great grief which droops the head of an elder', did not let him eat it.

Because it was much more plain to the Deputy now that 'when Death takes away the lives of our contemporaries, it is a warning for the rest of us to prepare for our turn'. The Deputy, Ọtun, knew now that whether sooner or later, he too would drive his brawling daughter away from his house in respect of her non-stop hot brawls.

So also for Kimi Adugbo, the Osi Ọba, grief did not let him eat and drink when he returned to his house that morning. For he was very sure now that there was no doubt. In a short time, he too would drive his wicked son, Alagẹmọ, away from his house.

It was not so long from when the Ọba drove his prince away, that the ex-prince was wandering all about in the town in very dirty rags. Having seen him in this total wretched condition, the elders to the youngest children of the town gave him a nickname that would fit his dirty and rough guise.

The nickname which the people gave him was Pauper, the Father of Wretchedness. But sometimes people called him Pauper or Father of Wretchedness. It was so his real name was forgotten entirely within a short time.

But one day, as Pauper, the Father of Wretchedness, was roaming about in the town he came to a ruined house, on the outskirts of the town. Having swept away all the refuse in it, he began to live in it.

When Pauper had just started to live in that ruined house, and as his poverty and wretchedness were so powerful, he had nothing to eat except those rotten remnants of food which were thrown into the dustbins and incinerators. But these did not satisfy his hunger at all.

But in the end, when Pauper had nearly died of hunger, by all means, he found the cutlass and hoe. Then he went into the bush. After he had cleared the bush, he made heaps. He sowed maize, pepper, vegetables, and he planted cassava and yams as well in those heaps.

One day, when he was returning from his farm to his house, he found one ripe orange on the roadside and he picked it up. After he had sucked the sweet juice in it, he brought the grains which were in that orange to the house. So he sowed two grains in front of the house, two at the back of the house and two on each side of the house.

Before long, those grains shot out and then Pauper started to tend them as they were growing further.

But after a few months, Pauper's crops were ripe enough and by that, he began to live on them satisfactorily.

Although his crops could have yielded far better than that. His poverty and wretchedness were so powerful in a strange way that they infected them badly. Every one of the crops was so infected that each of his yams was no bigger than an egg while there were no more than ten grains of corn on each cob. Even his pepper plants did not yield a single pepper at all.

In fact, however an ex-prince is poor and wretched, 'the remnants of the former royal blood will still remain in him'. For this reason, there were certain people who used to help Pauper, the Father of Wretchedness, sometimes with little money. But alas, the unfortunate destiny of Pauper used to repress all the supports which he used to receive from these people.

Worse still, as he was growing older thus his poverty and wretchedness were growing even worse than ever. Hereby, he could not get a lady who agreed to marry him. For old and young people of the town had already known him very well as they knew money, that it was in poverty and wretchedness he was dwelling every day.

It was like that Pauper continued to dwell in his miserable destiny which he chose from Creator when he was coming to earth.

# THE DAUGHTER OF THE ỌTUN ỌBA
# IS A BRAWLER

In this same Laketu town, the Ọtun who was next in rank to Ọba, was a very courteous chief. His cheerfulness was such that both adults and young people and as well children of the town loved him as a miser loves money. For this, uncountable people of the town used to come to his house to greet him. And he used to welcome them with smiles. And when they were leaving, he used to give each of his admirers several kinds of important presents.

This Ọtun Ọba, whose surname was Alagbanko, got many children, sons and daughters. But to put derision aside, his children were so beautiful that their beauty also glorified Laketu town in that century. They too were very courteous just like their father.

Yet 'the teeth of the dog which are curved, spoil it'. He too had a problem with one of his daughters as the Ọba had with his own.

Among the Ọtun Ọba's daughters, there was one who, though she was as beautiful as a peacock, she was as great a brawler who was ever born in Laketu town. Her brawls were so many and so strong that they did not even let her eat so much.

Once she had started her brawls, there was nobody who could stop her. If she started to brawl from morning, she would not stop till she fell asleep just for a few minutes when it was night.

Even, as 'it is with full force the kernel is taken out of its shell', it was exactly so for this brawling lady. Even as she was a habitual brawler, she used to brawl continuously also in her sleep.

As brawling was her second language, whenever she saw a

hen, she would brawl on it for many minutes. If a bird flew past her, she would brawl hotly on it for many minutes. There was nothing on earth on which she would not brawl.

But as it is 'the great grief which droops the head of an elder', is that it was a great sadness for the Ọtun Ọba, who was the father of this brawling lady. Her father used to warn her always to stop her brawls. But she would not because brawling had become her permanent habit.

As a matter of fact, it was a very deep great grief for the Ọtun, to see one of his daughters who chose but brawls from Creator. But of course, the Babalawo, the Ifa priest, who read the 'ẹsẹnt'aye' or the life of this brawling lady years ago, said that it was the hotful brawls which the Ọtun Ọba's daughter had chosen from Creator. And that in the long run, her father would drive her away from his house when he and his neighbours were fed up with his daughter's hurtful brawls.

However, it was like that that the Ọtun Ọba's daughter continued to grow up with her brawls.

As time went on, this lady's brawls were much more harmful in climax so that her parents and their neighbours were unable to hear any other words with their ears both day and night except the brawls of this lady.

But furthermore, 'one thing spoils "ajao", its arms are bigger than its thighs'. The harmful brawls which this lady was brawling at this time rendered her useless entirely, because there was not a young man who ever attempted to marry her. Her hurtful brawls scared away every one who intended to marry her.

In the end, when her father, the Ọtun Ọba, and his neighbours were entirely fed up with her brawls, one morning, and in great anger, her father closed up both his eyes and then he drove her away from his house.

It was like that this brawling lady was driven away by her father just as the Ọba had driven his prince, Pauper, the Father of Wretchedness, away from his Aafin, or palace, some years ago. But then this brawling lady became a vagrant and she started to wander and brawl continuously about in the town like a mad lady.

But before long and as she was roaming about in the town, the people of the town, old and young men and women and children as well, knew very well now that one of her brawls was 'a heavy load which falls on one who carries it'.

Having known her like that, they gave her a nickname immediately which was fit for her behaviour. The nickname which people gave her was BRAWLER, because her hot brawls were a strange fashion which the people had never heard in their lives.

## 4

## PAUPER MARRIES BRAWLER

It was not so long before Brawler was wandering about in the town, brawling hotly and perspiring profusely. And she did not get a young man who ever attempted to marry her.

One day, she and Pauper, the Father of Wretchedness, met each other in the vicinity of the town. Immediately both of them met, Pauper stopped her and without hesitation, he told her that he wished her to be his wife. But without thinking twice, Brawler replied that it was quite a long time since she had been looking for a man who could marry her.

Brawler said that she agreed to marry Pauper. But she had hardly agreed when she resumed her usual harmful brawls. Now, this means one who is looking for a wife finds one who is looking for an husband. So the wish of Pauper and that of Brawler were agreeable in the end.

But then Pauper told Brawler to follow him to his house and without refusing, Brawler started to follow him. But Pauper was soon surprised greatly to see that Brawler did not stop brawling for a moment as she was following him along.

After a while, Pauper was fed up with Brawler's continuous brawls. But then he stopped unexpectedly and Brawler stood in front of him without stopping her brawls. 'By the way, why are you brawling hotly like this?' in annoyance, Pauper asked from Brawler.

'Haaa, don't you know my name?' Brawler shouted.

'But what is your name?' Pauper fastened his eyes on Brawler and asked.

'Oh! pity, but Brawler is my name! With this name, the old and young men and women and even the children of the town are calling me!' Without shame, Brawler told Pauper her name.

'Brawler or what?' Pauper wondered and was startled in fear.

'Surely, Brawler is my name!' Brawler shrugged and replied fast and then she continued her brawls.

'Does that mean you cannot stop your brawls just for a few minutes and let your mind be at rest or how?' Pauper asked earnestly.

'Ha-a-a! That is impossible for me to do! So far "we cannot take the shape of the nose away from the nose", the brawls cannot be taken from me, hence brawls are my everyday work!' But Brawler had hardly explained herself to Pauper when she continued her brawls.

'Does that mean that "nothing can be done to prevent a pig from swimming in a swamp"?' Pauper asked greedily.

'Certainly! Did you not know that before today? By the way, what is your own name? Because it is proper for a wife to know the name of her husband!' Brawler remembered now to ask for the name of her husband, although she had not yet followed Pauper to his house.

'Pauper, the Father of Wretchedness, is my full name! Both young and old people of the town have given me this nickname!' Pauper told his brawling wife.

'Haaa!' Brawler was startled. 'But what have you called your name now and let me hear it again, Pauper or Riches?' Brawler was greatly surprised and sighed as she looked at Pauper sternly in her uncontrolled hot brawls.

'My name is not riches or wealth but I say it is Pauper. But sometimes many people call me the Father of Wretchedness, when they see that my poverty and wretchedness are so much and powerful that they are beyond the knowledge of human beings! In fact, I am a strong man who fights with the matchet!' Pauper told Brawler his biography briefly.

'Haaa! But you should admit that it is a very bad destiny which causes poverty and wretchedness for a person! Okay! But being as "the parrot is the bird of the sea; the woodcock the bird of lagoon. And when we eat we must not forget our solemn

13

promises". I have already agreed to marry you,' Brawler continued, 'my right is to fulfil my promise. I must not divorce you simply because you are in poverty and wretchedness. Or if I do so, it means I eat my promise together with my food!

'But,' Brawler went further, 'you Pauper, should know that as I endure your own poverty and wretchedness, it is so you too must endure my own abnormal character which is my brawls. Because there is "nothing can be done to the Ifa oracle to prevent it from behaving like the palm kernels". I cannot do without brawling hotly like the dead!' Brawler concluded her covenant. 'All right, as wife and husband, let us continue our journey to your house!'

Then Brawler followed her husband, Pauper, to his house. Truly, all of his neighbours knew well that Pauper was poor and wretched and that he was very strong and active. But it was too strange to them when they started to hear hurtful brawls suddenly in his house, whereas they had never heard such brawls in his house before this time.

For this reason, without hesitation and in horror, Pauper's neighbours rushed out and gathered in front of his house. Then all of them were looking at Brawler in amazement as she was brawling up and down in the house. But when Pauper went to the outside and he explained to them that Brawler was his wife and that she was not mad, but brawls were her main work, then his neighbours returned to their houses in wonder and shock.

Thus Pauper and his wife, Brawler, started to live together in poverty, wretchedness, brawls and fight. But as soon as it was daybreak, Brawler would start to sweep the house and both front and back of the house as she continued to brawl hotly. Meanwhile Pauper too would take his cutlass and hoe. He would go to his farm which was not so far from the house.

After he had worked on his farm and was tired, he would dig out some yams from the heaps and he would take some cobs of maize as well. Then he would carry them to the house. It was those yams and corn which he and his brawling wife would eat as their daily meal. It was so he was doing every day. Even though the yams and corn were not satisfying their hunger, the hot brawls of Brawler did not let her feel much hunger.

14

Pauper's yams and corn were so much infected by his powerful poverty and wretchedness that each of the yams was not bigger than an egg and so the grains of his corn were not more than ten or twenty grains on each cob.

But as time went on it was so Brawler's brawls were becoming more terrible and harmful. Although Pauper and Brawler were dwelling in poverty, wretchedness, brawls and fights, Pauper's niece from his mother's side, whose name was Alaafia or Peace, and Brawler's niece from her mother's side, whose name was Ayọ or Joy, came to live with them. Peace was about fifteen years old and so was Joy. Both Peace and Joy were very lowly, loyal, cautious and sinless young girls. They were going about every day, looking for only things which were peaceful and joyful.

But in the long run, and as time went on, the brawls which Brawler was brawling harmed Peace and Joy much. And when they could no longer endure the harmful effects which the brawls gave them, then they fled to one house which was near a big river. Both of them began to live in that house with great peace and joy.

Then hardly was it cock-crow in the morning when Brawler would start her usual hurtful brawls. But instead of forcing herself to stop her brawls, she took brawls as her everyday work now.

The days that her brawls so much intoxicated her, she would start to chase her husband about inside the house and from the backyard to the front of the house. And so also she would be chasing him about with hot brawls round their neighbourhood. It was so she would continue to do till nightfall when she would fall asleep unnoticed.

For this her fearful behaviour, she had no time to do a sort of work which could fetch her money. But of course 'what we like most forms the greater part of our possession'. Brawler was using her brawls just as her pride in the presence of people. She did not take brawls to be a bad thing at all.

Even their neighbours knew very well that there was no doubt, only Pauper and Brawler could live with each other.

But the worst thing was that the whole women of their neighbourhood hated Brawler entirely in respect of her non-stop brawls. Even their neighbours used to express it in their proverb that, 'demijohn is abusing bottle, whereas both of them are made from the same material, instead of co-operating as friends, they hate each other!' Their neighbours went further, 'Pauper is the first man in Laketu town whose poverty and wretchedness are above the knowledge of human beings. And so his wife, Brawler, is the first woman we have ever seen in this Laketu town whose brawls are above the knowledge of human beings! Ha-a! Alas, Brawler, whose beauty glorifies the town, is entirely devastated by her harmful brawls!' That was how their neighbours assessed Pauper and Brawler to be.

Later, the behaviours of Pauper and Brawler will be continued.

# 5

# THE OSI ỌBA DRIVES HIS SON
# AWAY FROM HIS HOUSE

The Osi Ọba is the title of the man who was third in rank to the
Ọba. His name was Kimi Adugbo. This Osi Ọba was a strong and
true-hearted man. He hated an unrighteous person indeed.

When a thief was caught in his neighbourhood, he never set
him free. But he would tell the strong young men to go and kill
him, and after to nail his head onto a big tree which was near the
road which went to the market, so that the people might learn a
lesson from it when they saw it. For this action, there was not a
thief who was brave enough to come to his neighbourhood.

As Kimi Adugbo, the Osi Ọba and who was the father of
Alagẹmọ, was very faithful, whenever people brought a case to
him for settlement, he never gave the right to one who was
wrong and so he never gave the wrong to one who was right. But
he would judge the case without any slight partiality. So for this,
the people of the town respected him indeed.

Truly, the Osi Ọba got many children, sons and daughters, as
well as the Ọba and the Otun Ọba got several children. But there
was one among his children whom he loved more than the rest.
This one was born on the third day of the month of Agẹmọ or
July.

But as the custom of Laketu town was, Kimi Adugbo, Osi Ọba,
consulted the Babalawo, the Ifa priest, to help him find out from
the Ifa the kind of destiny which his baby boy had chosen from
Creator before coming to earth.

The Babalawo asked from the Ifa through Ọpẹlẹ or the Ifa's
messenger and he explained to Kimi Adugbo that: 'This your
child will be a poor man whose kind we have not seen in this

Laketu town before.' The Babalawo continued his prophecy, he said: 'This your child will be a very powerful and merciless raider, an outlaw, an outrage, a traitor, a slanderer, a transgressor, a tricker, a criminal, a cunning person, a tale-bearer, a cheater, a burglar, a truant, a wild fellow, a great confusionist, etc., whose kind is very rare to see on earth!' the Babalawo said.

'That is that,' the Babalawo advanced in his prophecy as he was pointing his finger to the child, he said: 'Certainly, in respect of his evil character and wickednesses, in the end you will drive him away from your house as soon as he has attained the age of manhood. And moreover, after a while, when the Ọba and his chiefs have changed him to an immortal in the name of Creator, then they will expel him away from this Laketu town,' the Babalawo said. 'That is that,' the Babalawo went on in his prophecy, he said: 'This your child will be a wanderer. But in his wandering, he will wander to a faraway foreign town. The inhabitants of that town will install him their Ọtun Ọba!' The Babalawo went further, he said: 'But it is a pity indeed that after your boy has enjoyed much on his throne, by his cunnings, he will cause what will definitely dethrone him. But then, he will return to his former hostile behaviours.'

The Babalawo continued the 'ẹsẹnt'aye' or how the future of Kimi Adugbo's child will be. He said: 'And your child will continue to live in his hostile behaviour until he gets lost entirely in his wandering and nobody will see or meet him forever. In fact, nobody will see or meet him but he will be pestering the people on earth invisibly every day.'

The Babalawo concluded his prophecy, he said: 'But inasmuch as unforeseen evil is one of his bad behaviours, surely, he will use his same unforeseen evil characters to dethrone the Ọba whom he met on the throne in that faraway town!' It was like that the Babalawo, the Ifa priest, explained to Kimi Adugbo, the Osi Ọba, how the 'ẹsẹnt'aye' or what the future of his child would be.

But then it was 'the great grief which droops the heads of elders' for Kimi Adugbo when he heard the bad 'ẹsẹnt'aye' of his child that morning. He was so sad that his mouth rejected food and drink, and great depression overwhelmed him immediately.

Even the grief was overmuch for him so that he was unable to thank the Babalawo when he was leaving for his house that morning.

After a few days, however, Kimi Adugbo accepted his fate and then he continued to be as cheerful to the people as he was before the 'ẹsẹnt'aye' of his child was read to him.

When Kimi Adugbo's child became eight days old, he reluctantly gave him a name which was ALAGẸMỌ. The meaning of this name 'Alagẹmọ' is chameleon worshipper. But Kimi Adugbo named this his child in proverb, 'The Agẹmọ dancer said that he had done all he could to train his child how to dance. But if he does not know how to dance, that will be his fault.'

Moreover, his child was born in the month of Agẹmọ (July). But now it is known that the prince of Ọba chose the destiny of poverty and wretchedness, the daughter of the Ọtun Ọba chose the destiny of harmful brawls, while the boy of Kimi Adugbo chose the destiny of the multifarious evil characters from Creator before the three of them were coming to earth.

But according to the Babalawo's prophecy as Alagẹmọ was growing up it was so his characters were becoming more hostile. As soon as he had grown to manhood and as 'it is impossible for evil-doer to refrain himself from his wickedness', is that one night, after all people had slept deeply, Alagẹmọ woke up, he went out cautiously into the premises which belonged to one of the neighbours. He loosened the rope with which one big ewe was tightened onto a wooden skewer, ready to be taken to the market in the morning.

But then Alagẹmọ took the ewe to his father's premises and he tightened it onto a pillar there. After, he went back to his room. But his intention was to take the animal to the market in the morning and sell it. But when 'Esu' or devil deceived Alagẹmọ, he fell asleep, and it was already daybreak before he woke.

Now, 'the lion is in open plain, the light is shone on it'. It was just so for Alagẹmọ that morning. He could not take the ewe to the market, and so he could not return it into the premises from which he had stolen it.

But it was hardly daybreak when the owner of the animal

began to search here and there in the neighbourhood for her ewe. A little after, she started to hear her animal crying loudly in the premises belonging to Kimi Adugbo, the Osi Ọba, and he who was Alagẹmọ's father.

But 'in a wink of monkey', the owner of the animal went into the premises of Kimi Adugbo, and she found her animal there, tightened onto a pillar. But then without hesitation, she went direct to Kimi Adugbo. She complained to him that someone who had stolen her ewe had brought it into his premises. Hearing this, Kimi Adugbo was shocked and marvelled much so that he stood up at once. He followed the owner of the ewe to his premises.

He was overwhelmed by grief and shame entirely when he saw that it was true someone had tightened the ewe onto one pillar in his premises. But as 'good character is a pride to a person', is that the whole of the neighbours were very sure that Kimi Adugbo was not a thief at all. He hated thieves and robbers indeed. But they were sure that it was his son, Alagẹmọ the evil-doer, who stole the ewe overnight and brought it into his father's premises.

But if Kimi Adugbo had not been a true-hearted chief, thus his son would have put him in trouble. But when he punished his son severely, he confessed immediately that he was the one who stole the ewe in the mid-night.

But then without hesitation, and without mercy, Kimi Adugbo gave an order to the strong young men to go and kill Alagẹmọ, his son, in the same way that thieves were killed. But when the crowd of people appeased him for many minutes to pardon his son, he reluctantly agreed to their appeal so that those people might not take him to be an obstinate and self-willed chief.

Although Kimi Adugbo respected the people's appeal, in their presence and in great anger, he drove Alagẹmọ, his son, away from his house immediately. Because 'he who fears injuries should keep himself away from injurious things'.

Now, Alagẹmọ began to wander about in the town. A few days later, when the people knew well that the whole evil characters which were on earth were in him, both old and young people gave him a nickname which was SLANDERER, and thus his real name Alagẹmọ was soon forgotten.

20

As Alagẹmọ, who is now known as Slanderer, was roaming about in the town, it was so he began to behave wickedly to the people. Sometimes he would bring his fellow raiders to the town. They would steal other people's property and sell all at cheap prices. Sometimes, he would knowingly put people in serious trouble.

After a while, Slanderer saw one ruined house on the outskirts of the town. Then he began to live in it without fear. But of course he himself was fear of fears. This his ruined house was very close to one mighty iroko tree. But he was lucky that people used to bring sacrifices to this iroko tree often. Although the sacrifices were meant for the spirit which inhabited the tree, he was the one who used to eat those sacrifices for he was so lazy that he could not work for his daily living.

As years went on, it was so Slanderer's wickednesses were becoming worse than ever. For this, old, young and children of the town had no rest of mind any more, because he used to cause confusions in the town. But of course, Kimi Adugbo, his ex-father, was certain that everything which the Babalawo had foretold about Slanderer would come to pass on him.

# 6

## SLANDERER BECOMES
## A CLOSE FRIEND OF PAUPER

One evening, as Slanderer was going by the nooks and corners in the dark, looking for his dinner, because he was nearly dead from hunger at that time, for he was so lazy that he could not make farm, he met Pauper, the Father of Wretchedness, by chance. And Pauper was carrying one dead she-goat along to his house, from which he and his wife, Brawler, were going to eat as their dinner. That dead she-goat had been thrown in the incinerator and it had already swelled out to the state of bursting just in a few hours' time.

As Pauper was carrying this rotten animal along to his house, immediately Slanderer saw him. He shouted and greeted Pauper very well. Pauper too responded to his greeting with a lovely voice. Then Slanderer, with his cunnings, shouted to Pauper: 'My friend, put your dead she-goat on my head and let me help you carry it to your house!'

'O I thank you much! Come and help me carry it!' So Pauper put the dead animal on Slanderer's head. But as both of them were going along abreast, Slanderer asked Pauper for the part of the town in which he lived. Pauper replied that he was living on the outskirts of the town.

'It is on the outskirts of the town that I live too!'

'Which part?' Pauper asked.

'I live near a certain mighty iroko tree!'

'If that is so, my own house is not far from that iroko tree! That means we are the same neighbours then!' Pauper was happy that he at last got another neighbour.

Soon, Pauper and Slanderer came to his house. Then he told

Slanderer to put the dead she-goat down in front of the house. Then the two of them entered his house. He showed Slanderer every part of his house without knowing him before.

But Slanderer had a great shock when he first saw how Brawler, Pauper's wife, was brawling hotly up and down in the house so much that she was entirely soaked by her sweat.

'But who is this woman?' Slanderer asked in fear. 'Or you and a madwoman are living together?' Slanderer asked again in fear. 'Does she bite people?'

'O no! She does not bite at all! But she is simply brawling and she is my wife!' Pauper explained to Slanderer.

After, both of them returned to the front of the house. They burnt off the hair of the dead she-goat. And having cut it into pieces, Brawler, without stopping her brawls once, came to the outside. Having cooked some of it together with other kind of food, she served some of the meat to Pauper and Slanderer. But she could not eat that which she served herself much because of her harmful brawls. But Pauper and Slanderer ate their own to their satisfaction.

Soon after Pauper and Slanderer, his friend, had eaten from the dead she-goat, Slanderer asked him: 'What is your name, my friend?' For he had not known Pauper's name since they had met. But Pauper told him that the people of the town were calling him Pauper, the Father of Wretchedness. He explained further to Slanderer that the people gave him the name when they saw that his poverty and wretchedness were such that he was wearing only dirty rags about every day.

Pauper told Slanderer further that he was the prince of that Laketu town. He told him that in the long run the Ọba, his father, drove him away from his palace when he saw that the destiny which he chose from Creator was poverty and wretchedness. He explained to Slanderer that he did not believe at all that there was anything like destiny.

Pauper explained further to Slanderer that the Babalawo had foretold in his 'ẹsẹnt'aye' that he would become an Ọba in a faraway town. He again disclosed to Slanderer that of course his close friend's cunnings would dethrone him, but then he would return to his former poverty and wretchedness. It was like that Pauper related his story to his friend, Slanderer, that night.

'Thank you very much Pauper. I have heard all your story clean and clear. But what is forcing your wife to brawl hotly like that?' Slanderer asked from Pauper.

'Thank you very much, Slanderer. Just so we should ask. You see, my wife is the daughter of the Ọtun Ọba. But the day that the Babalawo read her 'ẹsẹnt'aye' or her destiny, the Ifa disclosed that she would be brawling throughout her lifetime on earth and that she would be fighting throughout her lifetime on earth, because she is destined mainly for all that!' Pauper told Slanderer further that: 'But when my wife's brawls were overmuch, then her father, the Ọtun Ọba, drove her away from his house. But one day, we met each other in our wandering in the town. Then I married her!' Pauper said.

'Hun-un!' Slanderer took a full breath. 'That means you, the husband's, destiny is poverty and wretchedness while that of your wife is brawls and fight?' Slanderer asked Pauper with his usual cunning.

'You are correct!' Pauper replied. 'But as for me, I don't believe in destiny at all!' Pauper shook his head.

'Now, I have told you all about myself, my friend. But I wish you to tell me your own story as well!' Pauper wanted to hear Slanderer's biography.

'Thank you very much, Pauper. It is so we should ask!' Slanderer started his own story, he said: 'As you, Pauper, are the ex-prince of this our Laketu town, and as the father of your wife is the daughter of the Ọtun Ọba. It is so my own father, Kimi Adugbo (the stronghold of neighbourhood) is Osi Ọba (left-hand man to the Ọba).'

Slanderer went on, he said: 'My father expelled me away from his house when he saw that the destiny which I chose from Creator was bad indeed. But it was not so long before the people of the town started to call me Slanderer instead of my real name, Alagẹmọ!'

Slanderer continued his biography, he said: 'The sorts of destiny which I chose from Creator are the evil characters, such

24

as raider, outlaw, outrage, truant, a wild fellow, sluggard, traitor, confusionist, a tale-bearer, a great cheater, double-dealer, plotter, etc. etc., just to mention a few. Because there are still other kinds of uncountable characters which are too terrible to hear, in my hand. And I behave as some of these evil characters every day!'

Slanderer went further, he said: 'Moreover, I am still looking for a chance to take revenge on my father, Kimi Adugbo, for the severe punishment which he gave me the day that I stole one ewe!'

'But why? You alone have all these kinds of evil characters? Haa! I am afraid, your evil characters are too many!' Pauper shouted suddenly in great zeal. And Brawler, too, shouted greatly at Slanderer with her hot brawls.

Slanderer went on in his biography, he told Pauper that: 'But of course the Babalawo had foretold to my father long ago that in my wandering I would reach a faraway town and the people of that town would install me their Ọtun Ọba!'

Slanderer shortened his biography, he told Pauper that: 'The Babalawo told my father further that, although it was a pity, after I had enjoyed much while on the throne, I would cause something by my cunnings which would dethrone me. And that my same cunnings would cause also the dethronement of the Ọba who was on the throne before I became his Ọtun. But then I would go back to my former distress and my horrible evil characters. But then I would continue my punishments all about until I would be vanished on earth!' Thus Slanderer told his biography in brief to Pauper that night.

# 7

## PAUPER AND SLANDERER DEBATE ON DESTINY

'But, anyway, I have not even a slight belief that there is something which is called destiny!' Pauper shook his head to left and right. He made it clear to Slanderer.

'Haaa! Pauper, don't say so any more! Really, there is destiny! Hoo, that means you don't understand that your poverty and wretchedness are your destiny?' Slanderer made Pauper understand that destiny existed, as he looked at him sternly.

'Nevertheless I shall not believe that my poverty and wretchedness are my destiny!' Pauper disagreed entirely.

'That means you don't know that my destiny is my wicked characters with which I behave to people every day? Answer me, Pauper!' Slanderer tried to make Pauper believe that destiny existed.

'I repeat it with confidence, there is no destiny at all!' Pauper shouted to Slanderer in great anger.

'I say it again and I confirm it again, there is destiny!' Slanderer shouted to Pauper in passion.

'But I do not agree with you at all! There is nothing as such!' Pauper shouted in uncontrolled anger.

Now, both friends stood up. In anger, they were pointing fingers to each others' faces, as they were perspiring continuously.

'I shall never believe in anything which is uncertainty!' Pauper pushed Slanderer's nose with a finger.

'All right! All right! That is all right! Just take it cool!' Slanderer called Pauper to order.

'All right, Slanderer, throw more light on destiny!' Pauper said, and then he hesitated.

'All right, Pauper, tell me why your father, the Ọba, expelled you from his Aafin?'

'Yes, my father expelled me in respect of my poverty and wretchedness when they are more complicated than human knowledge!'

'Oh well! Okay, it isn't bad yet. But let us suspend our debate on destiny for another time, because a furious debate as this one spoils friendship. But sooner or later, when we start our endless journey, according to what the Ifa had foresaid, then it will be clear to you that there is no doubt, destiny exists, and that it rules every human being. And moreover, you will understand well that it is your destiny which is troubling you so much that you are wearing only rags all about every day!' Slanderer said.

'All that the Ifa,' Slanderer continued, 'had said about one's 'ẹsẹnt'aye' will never fail but it will come to pass!' It was like that Slanderer reminded Pauper of all that the Ifa had said about them in the past. And then they suspended their furious debate.

They sat back without wrestling with each other, because Slanderer was lazy and he could not fight. But of course, 'when there is no third person, that is why two persons fight to death'. But the worst of it was that Brawler who was the third person among Pauper and Slanderer, should have been the mediator for them. But her continuous hot brawls did not let her pay heed to the hot debate which caused the quarrel between Slanderer and Pauper.

When it was time to sleep, Pauper and Slanderer entered the room and they slept. Even if Brawler's brawls interfered with Slanderer's sleep so much that he was unable to sleep well, yet he was happy that he and Pauper had become close friends.

In the morning and after both friends had eaten from the dead she-goat with other food, Pauper followed Slanderer to his house but he did not keep so long before he returned to his house. Thus the two friends were visiting each other every day. But being as Slanderer had no food in his house to eat, he was lucky that he got it in Pauper's house every time.

But as it is 'what will happen to someone makes him senseless', is that Pauper trusted Slanderer heartily without knowing that he was an entirely unforeseen evil-doer and a great traitor.

But, as I have said earlier, Pauper sowed two grains of orange in front and back and also two each on both sides of his house. As soon as the trees grew up they started to bear oranges. Each of the trees yielded one hundred oranges every year. Even though Pauper's poverty and wretchedness were so powerful that they were infecting all of his crops so much that they were unhealthy and each was as small as an egg, the oranges which those trees yielded were very good and their sweetness was much better than all other oranges in Laketu town. As they were so sweet, all Pauper's neighbours used to come to him every time and ask him to give them some to suck.

# 8

## CREATOR SENDS HIS IKQ
## TO PAUPER AND BRAWLER

Just as Pauper, the Father of Wretchedness, and his wife, Brawler, continued to live in poverty, wretchedness, brawls and fight, Creator saw them and He was much filled with pity for their unrest of minds, so that one morning he sent one of His Ikǫ or messengers to them, to ask from each of them the kind of help which he or she wished Him to do for him or her, although their destiny would not miss them.

So the Ikǫ came down to their town, Laketu. As soon as he walked zigzag in the town, he came to their doorway and then he stopped there. But being as 'it is the sender of a message the messenger should fear and not to whom he is sent', for this, without fear, Creator's Ikǫ began to knock at Pauper's door and with respect, he was greeting loudly: 'Good morning to you here! Good morning to all here.'

'Good morning to you! Please come in!' Pauper responded, but poverty and wretchedness showed clearly in his voice. But Brawler's hot brawls did not let her hear that somebody was knocking at their door.

However, Creator's Ikǫ entered the house. When he stood in front of Pauper with smiles, he shouted: 'Creator sends a message of happiness to you, Pauper and your wife, Brawler!'

'Creator sends a message of happiness to me and my wife or what?' Pauper was greatly startled and then he moved back a bit from the Ikǫ before he asked.

'Certainly, Creator has sent a good message to you and your wife!' Creator's Ikǫ confirmed with a smile.

'But who are you?' in fear and trembling, Pauper asked. But of course, the hot brawls of his wife which forced her to go here and there in the house did not let her pay heed to the discussion which was going on between her husband and the Ikọ.

'I am one of Creator's Ikọ!'

'Hoo-o! Is that so! But what kind of message is it which Creator has sent to my wife and me?' Pauper asked in zeal and in his usual voice of poverty and wretchedness.

'Please, call your wife to come to us because the message concerns her as well!' the Messenger told Pauper and after, he hesitated, and then he looked on.

'Brawler! Brawler! Brawler! Please come and listen to the message which Creator has sent to us!'

'Yes, I am this! But what kind of message is it which Creator has sent to us?' Brawler pushed her chest forward and asked in a hurry. But then she continued her brawls at once.

'By the way, what makes you brawl harshly like this and your mouth is not tired, you a beautiful woman like this?' in astonishment, the Ikọ asked from Brawler. After, he folded both his arms across his chest, he hesitated and then he was looking on surprisedly.

'You see, the Messenger of Creator, there is no pleasure at all in the life of my husband. Instead, he dwells in both poverty and wretchedness. And the worse of it he is sluggish more than the bird which is called "sọ" and which is so sluggish that it cries once in a year!' Brawler explained to the Messenger with hot brawls.

'Does that mean you are brawling both day and night because your husband is in poverty and wretchedness, and that he is sluggish more than "sọ" the bird that cries once a year?' the Messenger teased Brawler with marvel.

'That is not so at all! Pauper is my husband. I know him very well as everyone knows money! His poverty and wretchedness are so strong that they infect whatever he plants on his farm! And moreover,' Brawler continued, 'all the people of the town hate him more than dung in respect of the dirty rags which he is wearing about every day!' But Brawler had hardly explained to the Messenger with fretfulness when she continued her brawls on another matter which entirely digressed from the complaints which she had made to Creator's Ikọ.

But then Creator's Ikọ breathed out heavily: 'Hun-un! That means you and your husband have identical characters which are indeed different from that of mankind.' The messenger or Ikọ continued to appease Brawler's anger: 'Because as you have accused your husband of his poverty and wretchedness, it was so he too accused you of your harmful and non-stop brawls! Therefore, I take both of you just like the bottle and demijohn which are accusing each other!'

The Ikọ went further in his appeasement, he told Brawler that: 'The bottle abuses the demijohn that it is made from the glass. And so the demijohn abuses the bottle as well that it is made from the glass. But what is the difference between glass and glass?' Thus the Ikọ appeased Brawler in proverb.

'Just so! I agree with you that the bottle and demijohn relate to each other!' Brawler replied with brawls.

'Hooo! It will be better for you, Brawler!' Creator's Ikọ went on in his appeasement, he said: 'As your husband is habitually a poor, wretched and ragged man, and that he is foolish much more than the bird called "sọ" which cries but only once in a year, and that it is certain that you are a pretty brawling woman who brawls harmfully on the whole things which are on earth, it is certain then that you and your husband have come to earth through the same "odu" (the indication of divination by the Ifa oracle)!' It was so the Ikọ of Creator appeased Brawler in a trickish way.

'All right, Brawler, what kind of help do you wish Creator to do for your husband?' the Ikọ asked from Brawler with a cool voice.

'Haaa! This is the happiest day for me since I came to earth! The kind of help that I wish Creator to do for my husband is to slay him for me! That is the only help I want from Him!' Brawler jumped up with happiness and shouted, as she was looking at her husband and the Ikọ with half an eye.

'Is that your wish?' the Ikọ asked in a shocked voice.

'Surely, that is what I want!' Brawler confirmed her wish as her husband was looking on speechlessly.

31

'That means you don't wish Creator to help you get money and child and further to relieve you of your harmful brawls but to slay your husband for you?' the Ikǫ asked Brawler whether she would repent from killing her husband.

'Haaa! Not at all! I have nothing to do with money or child or with being delivered from my brawls!' Brawler insisted mercilessly.

'Well! Okay!' the Ikǫ said. 'Please listen to me now, Pauper. But what kind of help do you wish Creator to do for your wife?' the Ikǫ turned his face to Pauper and asked him.

'Well, even though I am the one whose poverty and wretchedness are overmuch on earth in this century, and that my wife's brawls are the most peevish and that harmful uncountably to the people, and that my treasures on this earth are not more than the orange trees which surround my house and also the dirty rags which are on my body,' Pauper continued his request, he told the Ikǫ, 'but the most important thing that I wish Creator to give me is the power which is above all powers. That is one. The second one is to give to my voice a command which is so powerful that if a person touches my orange trees and if I command it, that person should stick onto the trees and immediately he should stick onto them!' Pauper went further in his request, he said: 'Please, Creator's Messenger, those are the kinds of powers that I wish Creator to give me!' Thus Pauper requested all that he wanted very carefully.

But of course, 'if a young man is just trying to behave like an old man, his age will not give him the way'. In fact, Pauper was so poor and wretched that his poverty and wretchedness were much beyond that of human knowledge. But he did not want the death of anybody like his wife.

'All right, it is not bad. But I will tell Creator, when I return to Him, the kind of help that which you, the husband, want from Him, and that which your wife wants Him to do for her! Goodbye!' the Creator's Ikǫ promised Pauper and his wife. But then he left their house and soon after, he was vanished from their view.

But when the Ikǫ returned to Creator, he told Him the kind of helps which Pauper and his wife, Brawler, wanted from Him. But without hesitation, Creator commanded that: 'Let the wish of Brawler be for her according to her wish. And let Pauper have the power of powers according to his wish. But it is not yet time to give to his voice the power of command!' Creator said.

Truly, immediately Creator approved one of Pauper's requests and He shelved the other one aside, power of command, for the other time. A power which was above all powers came to his body. He was stronger than a giant now. And for his wife, Brawler, Creator agreed to send Death to slay her husband, Pauper, for her.

Although Creator approved Brawler's wish, He could never be so cruel to those creatures whom He had created with His own hand. And He knew well that 'an elder who is over-doing things loses respect'. So He waited to see whether Death would be able to slay Pauper for his wife.

# 9

## DEATH ARRIVES TO SLAY PAUPER
## FOR HIS WIFE

One morning, when Pauper, the Father of Wretchedness, was wording his wife, Brawler, bitterly and sorrowfully, and his wife was wording him in return with different kinds of bitter brawls, and as both were chasing each other about inside and outside of the house; just then, Death, the slayer of mankind, arrived at their house unexpectedly. Without wasting one second, he shouted horribly to both of them, he said: 'Heee! Let you stop there! But you, Pauper, at your wife's wish, I come to slay you for her, just as Creator has instructed me to do!'

'I thank you indeed, Death, Father of Terror. With great respect, I agree with you to slay me for my wife's wish!' Pauper continued, he told Death, 'Even I have prepared to die this morning! Because I am willing greatly to go and meet all my ancestors in Creator's residence, where people go but do not return!' Pauper told Death without fear, even though the guise of Death, the killer of wealthy and poor people, was extremely terrifying.

Pauper went on, he told Death, the most cruel on earth, 'But I beg you indeed to do an obligation for me before you take my life!' Pauper implored Death with respect and without fear.

'But what kind of obligation do you wish me to do for you?' Death shouted terribly to Pauper. But as Death continued his horrible shout to Pauper, now, Brawler was extremely happy. But this time, she began to tiptoe round her husband and Death. She was despising her husband, saying that: 'Hun-hun-un! Death has caught you with his hands this day! Today is the last day for you to remain on earth!'

Brawler continued her derision, she said: 'A poor and wretched man you are!'

'Thank you much, Death,' Pauper continued his request: 'Do you see those orange trees, around my house?' he pointed his hand to the trees and showed them to Death.

'Yes, I see them!' Death looked and fastened his terrible eyes on the trees. 'But I have nothing to do with your orange trees. But just prepare yourself to surrender your life for your wife's wish!' Death shouted horribly. But Pauper was not afraid at all. Because Pauper was sure that 'without killing an animal, we cannot use its leather for making the drum'.

'I am grateful, Death. Those orange trees are the only property I have on earth. But of course, the second one which I have is the dirty rags with which I cover my body.' Pauper went on, he said: 'For this reason, I beg you to give me just a few minutes to pluck two oranges from the top of my trees; to suck them first before you slay me for my wife!' with lowliness, Pauper appealed to Death, the gigantic killer of people of earth.

But as Pauper was appealing to Death, his wife, Brawler, with great joy, began to cackle like a hen, and so she began to laugh with her gullet – 'kaa-kaa!' For she believed that, unfailingly, Death would slay her husband for her that morning. But Death refused Pauper's request, Death was able to turn down Pauper's request, simply because Creator had not yet given power of command to his voice. He (Creator) shelved it for some time to come.

Instead of granting Pauper's request, Death grappled his head with both his hands. But just as he tried to strangle him to death, Pauper too hastily grappled Death's thick neck. He started to use the strange power which Creator had given to his body and with it he tried to twist Death's neck.

Now, having felt much pain, willing or not, Death released Pauper's head when he wanted to break his neck. But then this time Death began to wrestle fiercely with Pauper. He attempted to lift him off the ground and then knock him to death. But 'it is the ceiling that bears the load; the shelf is only boasting'. Pauper did not let Death lift him off the ground. Therefore, all Death's efforts failed, he was just boasting.

Pauper attempted also to lift Death off the ground and knock him onto the ground. But for him, it was just 'a single hand which cannot lift up a full-loaded calabash onto the head'. He was unable to lift Death up. Therefore all his efforts failed as well.

As Death and Pauper continued their fierce fight and were trampling all the pots, ladles, basins and calabashes which were in Pauper's house into pieces with their feet, Brawler simply behaved now like 'the proud pond which stands aloof from the stream as though it is not related to the stream'. It was just so with Brawler that morning. Instead of parting the two fighters, she stood aloof and then she left them for their fate, as if she was not the one who had caused this scuffle.

But when it seemed to Brawler that Death wanted to over-power Pauper, she was so happy this time that she began to shout: 'Death, put more efforts and slay Pauper for me! Slay him in time!'

Thus Brawler continued to encourage Death with great joy but 'in a wink of monkey', Pauper and Death had fought from the house to the outside. But they continued their wrestling from there along to the town as they were entirely wet by their perspiration. Their feet were shooting dust high up till when they wrestled into the centre of the town.

The dust had so much covered both of them that the people could hardly see them in it. Having seen them fighting terribly, the people were so much afraid and confused that they began to shout greedily: 'Haaa! See Pauper, he is wrestling with a powerful Eṣu or Devil!' And so many others were shouting earnestly and with fear that: 'Pauper is fighting with an underworld being!'

But the people were still in great panic when another more terrible thing happened in the town unexpectedly at this very time.

This incident was that this very morning, Slanderer, the close friend of Pauper, brought countless of his fellow raiders to the town. All of them began to cause great confusion to every part of the town. They were breaking into the houses of the people. They were carrying their money and valuable property away. But soon, Pauper, Death, Slanderer and his fellow raiders became the terrors of the town.

The people were so confused and panic-stricken that it was not so long before mothers did not know where their children were. The husbands did not know where their wives were and so for their wives. It was like this Pauper, Death, Slanderer and his fellow raiders put the people and the town in great chaos that morning.

After all, when Death fought terribly with Pauper but was unable to slay him, they fought back to the front of Pauper's house. Now, Death was entirely tired and he was greatly thirsty, but Pauper was not tired, because the strange power which was above all powers which Creator had granted him suppressed Death's power, though he was the terror of terrors.

Death sat down in front of Pauper's house and he began to breathe in and out heavily for tiredness, at this time, Pauper stood up. He walked to one of his orange trees. But as he stretched out his right arm and he plucked two oranges from the branch of that tree, and then he started to suck one of the two, Death too stood up tiredly. He went to that orange tree.

But this time, Pauper kept silent but he was keeping watch on him with half an eye. But as Death stretched his hand up to the branch of the orange tree, and just to pluck one orange to suck it as Pauper did, just at this very time Creator sent the power of command to his voice. Then he commanded unexpectedly, he shouted: 'Death, let your arms and body stick on to my orange tree!'

To Death's fear and surprise, Pauper had hardly commanded like that when Death's body and hands stuck on to the orange tree. It was just like that the power of command which Creator had given to Pauper's voice worked miraculously now.

Just as 'the proud pond stands aloof from the stream as though it is not related to the water', it was like that for Brawler now, who had originated this great disaster. She stood aloof now and then she was looking at Death instead of going and helping him.

Although, Brawler was a foul-mouthed woman and who had been shouting to Death joyfully before to slay Pauper, her husband, for her, she was now so depressed that she was not aware when she opened her mouth in shock and the spit was dropping onto the ground. And so she began to doubt now whether Death would be able to slay her husband for her. But what happened to Death now was different from what she and Death himself expected.

Now, Death, the terror of human beings, had no more power in him immediately his hands and body had stuck on to the orange tree. He feared so much now that he started to beg Pauper in an earnest voice to command his orange tree to release him.

'What? To release you without a covenant? No!' Pauper was sulky and frowned at Death, the slayer of mankind.

'But what kind of covenant do you want from me?' Death asked in trembling mind.

'Unless you swear that as from today and for ever, you Death will not slay Pauper and Brawler. But then my orange tree will release you!' Pauper shouted to Death.

Now, it is just that, 'one should not ask the causes of his father's death but when he has seized the hilt of his sword'. But Pauper's hand had seized the hilt of sword now and then he was bold enough to ask 'the causes of his father's death' from Death.

Now, whether Death liked it or not he swore to Pauper that: 'Well, okay! As you, Pauper, have told me to do, I, Death who am ruining the houses of the wealthy people and also poor people by killing them, swear to you that as from today and on, I, Death will never kill Pauper and Brawler!' Death continued his covenant in fretfulness, 'Or if I attempt to do so, let the day change to night and let the darkness of the night swallow me up!'

But then as soon as Death had sworn to Pauper, he commanded his orange tree to release Death. But he feared Pauper so much now that he did not even wait and thank him before he fled and soon he was vanished.

But when Brawler was sure that Death had failed to slay her husband for her, she collapsed and then she fainted. Although Pauper knew well that all she wanted was his death, he started to treat her at once till she was conscious.

Brawler was hardly conscious when she stood up and then she

38

began to brawl persistently. But soon after, when Pauper was fed up with listening to her hot brawls, he started to speak to her rudely. And a few minutes later, their noises had filled up the house. But as they continued to abuse each other, Brawler's brawls began to intoxicate her so much that she started to bite her husband like a dog.

But when Pauper saw that his body began to bleed repeatedly, in panic, he fled to the outside and then he began to run as fast as he could to another part of the outskirts of the town, where there was a large river. But Brawler started to chase him along immediately to bite him again.

But before long, Brawler pursued her husband fiercely to the front of the house in which Peace and Joy lived by the side of the town. But we should remember that Peace or Alaafia was a relative of Pauper's mother, while Joy or Ayọ was a relative of Brawler's mother. They had both lived with them for some years, but later, they had quitted their house in great sadness, because these two lasses could not live together with quarrelsome persons.

Just as Brawler chased her husband to the front of the house in which Peace and Joy lived with rest of mind, she saw them standing at their doorway. Then with harsh brawls, she shouted to them: 'Please, Joy, help me bite my husband! Please, I beg you!'

'Haa! never shall I bite a person! I am Joy and I do only things which are joyful!' thus Joy declined to help Brawler bite her husband.

'Well, it is not bad yet! But Peace, please help me bite my husband, he is running away!' Brawler waved hands and shouted to Peace hurriedly.

'No! I shall not bite a person! But I do only peaceful things!' Thus Peace and Joy refused to help Brawler. But instead they hastily entered their house in which they lived in peace and joy which had no end.

After a while, Brawler chased Pauper, her husband, to the place where the town terminated. But the large river which was at the termination of the town disturbed Pauper from keeping on running along. So he hastily turned back and with restlessness of mind he continued to run into the town direct, with the hope that as he did so, his wife would stop chasing him.

But as it is for 'he who carries fire in his hand cannot wait', it was just so for Brawler that day. She did not stop or go back from her husband, but she continued to chase him along fiercely as she was brawling hotly.

It was not so long after Brawler was chasing Pauper about in the town, that thousands of people saw them and they were following them with great noise because the monstrous attitude of the couple was strange and terrible to them.

But as the fight of Brawler and her husband was going on in the town, the terrible scuffle of Slanderer and his fellow raiders was also going on in the town. But when these confusions were overmuch, to save their lives, the people began to flee in panic to the towns which surrounded this Laketu town. And very soon there were only a few people who remained in the town.

# 10

# THE EXPULSION OF PAUPER, BRAWLER
# AND SLANDERER FROM THE TOWN

In the long run, the Ọba and his chiefs believed that, if the scuffle and confusion which were going on in the town continued for a few minutes more, the town would be no longer existing. And moreover what terrified them much was that this very day was Ọjọ-Ẹti (The Day of Trouble – Friday), in the month of Ṣẹrẹ or January.

But as 'it is risky for one to go to bed while the roof is on fire', so, without hesitation, the Ọba and his chiefs ordered their royal policemen and the hunters of the town to go and arrest and bring to them Pauper, Brawler, and Slanderer and his fellow raiders.

As soon as they were brought to the Aafin or palace, Slanderer's fellow raiders escaped with the looted property. The Ọba ordered the royal policemen again to lead them to the strange rock which was on the outskirts of the town. The Ọba and his chiefs followed them immediately.

Having taken them to the front of the rock, they set the three of them in one row, in front of the huge hole which came through to the outside of the rock. But as the Ọba and chiefs stood in front of these offenders, Pauper, Brawler and Slanderer, for a few minutes, they heard from the huge hole a strange voice which shook the forest heavily and the town horribly.

Now, the Ọba and chiefs knew that Creator was ready to listen to the accusation that which they brought before Him, although the Ọba, his chiefs and spectators did not see Creator with their eyes. The Ọba said in His hearing that: 'Ye Creator of above and beyond earth, we bring these three offenders before You. The offence which they committed is that they put Laketu town in

41

scuffle and confusion so much that the people are fleeing with restlessness of mind to hide themselves in other towns.'

The Ọba continued, 'For this serious offence which these three offenders have committed, I, the Ọba of Laketu town, will curse upon each of them in Your hearing now! And I beseech Thee to approve of my cursings!'

After the Ọba had thus explained in anger to Creator, he turned his face to Pauper, the Father of Wretchedness, Brawler and Slanderer. But then he read their offence to them, that: 'You Pauper, you Brawler and you Slanderer, the three of you have put great confusion and scuffle in Laketu town!' The Ọba continued his accusation as he pointed his left hand to the three offenders. He shouted in greed: 'In the name of Creator, I, the Ọba of Laketu town hereby curse upon you that you Pauper and Brawler, that peace and joy will be scarce in your fold. But you Pauper and you Brawler will be chasing each other fiercely and in anger and brawls henceforth!'

'It is so all will be for them!' the chiefs shouted.

'Kango! Kango! Kango!' the Ọba's Bell-ringer sealed the Ọba's cursings with his bell.

The Ọba went on in his cursings, he shouted greedily: 'I curse upon you also that as from today which is Ọjọ-Ẹti, and in the month of Ṣẹrẹ both of you have become immortals! Let Creator put His approval on this my cursings! Thus it will be for you!'

It was like that the Ọba, in great anger, cursed upon Pauper and Brawler, his wife, that bitter day. But to the greatest wonder of those who were with the Ọba at this strange rock, the Ọba had hardly shouted his cursings to the end when they heard an enormous voice inside the huge hole, which shook the forest and wilderness in extreme fear. And it said: 'Yes, just so it will be for them! I have put my approval on your cursings!'

Hereafter, the Ọba turned his face to Slanderer. He pointed his left hand to him. Then he shouted loudly and greedily, he said: 'You, Slanderer, just as the whole of the evil characters which are on earth are in your hands, and as by your evil characters you have put Laketu town into serious chaos!' The Ọba continued, 'In the name of Creator, I, the Ọba of Laketu town hereby curse

42

upon you this day which is Ọjọ-Ẹti and in the month of Ṣẹrẹ, peace, happiness and rest of mind will be scarce for you! But you will be in a state of bitter chaos in your endless days on earth. And so you will continue to dwell in sufferings, distresses and hunger! But just as "the madman arranges his load unevenly", thus you will continue to behave with all your evil characters unevenly to all parts of the earth!'

'Furthermore,' the Ọba went further in his cursings, 'I curse upon you that you have become an immortal as from this bitter day! Moreover, you Slanderer, you Pauper, and you Brawler, will be wandering about until the three of you will disappear on earth in the end! As "a running horse does not look at its back", it is so the three of you will be running forward without returning to this Laketu town henceforth and forever!'

The Ọba continued his cursings: '"We see only the going of the water-flies but we don't see their return!" It is your leaving that we shall see and not your return! Let Creator approve these my cursings!'

But then the Ọba's chiefs, with one voice, shouted in greed: 'It is so all will be for them!'

'Kango! Kango! Kango!' The Ọba's Bell-ringer hastily sealed the cursings with his bell.

But the Ọba had hardly cursed upon Pauper, Brawler and Slanderer to the end when a strange, fearful voice roared and it said: 'It is so all will be for them! I have put my approval on your cursings.'

Hereafter, the Ọba filled a bowl to its brim with the water of the pond of antiquity which was in front of the huge hole. He poured it onto the heads of Pauper, Brawler and Slanderer.

After, the Ọba told them in great passion: 'The three of you have become immortals as from today. Now, it is time for you to start your endless journey! So our meeting is indefinitely in dreams only or perhaps also on the road! Goodbye to you all!'

But the Ọba had hardly bade them goodbye when the royal policemen, with their batons, started to drive them away from Laketu town. The reason for driving them out of the town immediately was that the Ọba and his chiefs believed that the ancient water which was poured onto them must not dry off from their bodies while they were still in the town. Otherwise there would be an epidemic disease like influenza in the town that year and by that many people would die.

It was like that Pauper, the Father of Wretchedness, Brawler, his wife, and Slanderer left Laketu town that day which was Ọjọ-Ẹti and they started their endless and unreturnable journey.

But in fact as 'a predicted war does not affect a lame person', because he will go and hide himself in a safe place before the war comes, it was just so for Pauper, Brawler and Slanderer. The Ifa had predicted on the third day of their birth that, according to the destiny which each of them had chosen from Creator, they would be expelled from the town in the end. This means the prediction of the Ifa had come to pass upon them. Therefore, their expulsion from the town was not new to them. But alas, Pauper did not believe yet that destiny exists.

As soon as Pauper, Brawler and Slanderer had been driven away, the Ọba called Peace, who was related to Pauper's mother, and Joy, who was related to Brawler's mother. He told the two sinless girls that: 'You Peace and you Joy, in the name of Creator and in great joyful and peaceful mind, I change you from mortals to immortals as from this day which is Ọjọ-Ẹti, in the month of Ṣẹrẹ. So you Peace, are no longer the relation of Pauper's mother. And so you Joy, are no longer the relation of Brawler's mother as from today!'

The Ọba went on in his order, he told them: 'And henceforth, it is forbidden for the two of you to live in the house and town in which there are poverty, brawls, slander, chaos, panic, confusion and evil-doers!' The Ọba went further in his order, he told them: 'But the sort of people with whom you should live are people of good character, painstaking people, righteous people, and people who are meek. Those are the sort of people you should be seeking for in every part of the earth. And you should be peaceful and joyful to them! Let Creator approve this my order!'

But as the Ọba had given the order to Peace and Joy like that, Creator shouted greatly. He said: 'Yes, it is so all will be for them!' But when the Ọba and Creator had given orders to Peace and Joy like that, they went on their way at once.

But then, the Ọba, his chiefs, his royal policemen and uncountable people of the town, went back to the town. So as from that day peace had started to reign in Laketu town.

# 11

# PAUPER AND SLANDERER GO TO ABALABI TOWN

Immediately Pauper, the Father of Wretchedness, Brawler, his wife, and Slanderer were driven out of their town shamefully as offenders, the three of them began to run along on the road helter-skelter, without looking at their back. This road went to a town called Abalabi. This town was very far away from Laketu town.

It was not so long that they were running along. But as Death had failed to slay Pauper for his wife according to her wish, and as that was a great sorrow to her, after a while, and as she continued to brawl hotly along the road like a dead, she grasped Pauper suddenly. But as she wanted to bite him, he snatched himself away from her, and without hesitation he began to run along at a furious pace for his life. And Slanderer, too, followed him.

But as 'unsteadiness is dance', Brawler did not stop but she began to chase them along. But she could not overtake them until they had disappeared on the road. As 'it is with carefulness that a wise man runs away from a bull', so Pauper ran away from his hostile wife that day with carefulness.

Not so long after, Pauper and Slanderer ran helter-skelter to one crossroads. Several roads met at this crossroads. But without stopping there, Pauper and Slanderer ran to the road which went westward and there they continued running along.

But when Brawler ran to the crossroads in anger and hot brawls, she stopped there, because she did not know which of the roads her husband and Slanderer took so that she might continue to chase them along that road.

This crossroads was indeed to Brawler proof that 'the place where three roads meet puzzles a stranger'. Brawler was so confused that she did not know which of the roads she should take. Having brawled hotly for many minutes at the crossroads, she took the road which went eastward. She thought that was the right one which her husband took. But of course, 'when Creator wants to punish a dog, He will put sore on its forehead'. It was just so for Brawler that day.

She ran and ran on that wrong road till the darkness of the night was approaching. But alas, all her efforts and hope had failed. She did not see with her eyes one who even resembled her husband at all. But when she became tired and wearied, she stopped on the roadside, and in great anger she brawled so hotly that her brawls of that moment were as hot as boiling water which was still on fire. Yet, she did not see her husband.

But it was a pity that Brawler travelled on this wrong road for three days before she came to a small town called Ṣodeji. But being extremely exhausted, this forced her to break her journey in that town. She lodged in the house of a middle-aged woman. But every morning she used to go to the market, near that town, thinking that probably she would see her husband there. But 'shelf is just telling a lie, the loads belong to the ceiling'. Brawler simply deceived herself, her husband was not there.

Now to continue Pauper's adventure. When he and his close friend, Slanderer, ran and ran on the road which went westward, in the long run, they came to a town whose name was Abalabi. Pauper and Slanderer put up in a house there. But Pauper did not go out of the house for some days, because he feared perhaps his wife was in that town and saw him. He was not aware that she had mistakenly gone to the eastward.

However, when Pauper was thoroughly sure that Brawler was not in Abalabi town, he started to go out and walk freely about in the town. Now, this means Pauper was in the west while his wife was in the east.

Inasmuch as Pauper was a very hard-working man, sensible, cheerful and enduring, although his poverty and wretchedness were punishing him severely, all these helped him so much that several young men of his age became friendly with him very soon.

One of his friends taught him the art of wood-carving of different kinds such as images of masquerades, images of the noble people, domestic utensils, etc.

It was like that Pauper became an expert wood-carver. And it was so Pauper's manner of living went in this town. But he was afraid sometimes whenever he remembered his wife. His fear was that it was possible for her to come to Abalabi town and see him.

Further, he was certain that he and Brawler must come together again. Because the Ọba of Laketu town, his father, had cursed upon the two of them in the name of Creator that wherever he was, Brawler would be there with him. And wherever Brawler was, he would be there with her. Although they might be parted, that would be just for a short time.

But what kind of work was that which Slanderer was doing since he and Pauper had come to Abalabi town? In fact he was so lazy that he could neither till the ground nor could he clean the road. He was even so lazy that it was hard for him to put the morsels of his food into his mouth by himself.

But he had various kinds of cunnings with which he used to put people in trouble and he was a strong tale-bearer for the Ọba and his chiefs in Abalabi town. For this, they loved him indeed.

When Pauper had been qualified in wood-carving, one morning, he went into the forest. He felled one big tree. Having cut it into the sizes that he required, then he carved them into various kinds of images and domestic utensils. All were so beautiful that the people rushed to buy them immediately he carried them to the town.

Everything which Pauper carved from wood was so beautiful that his fame soon went round Abalabi town and to all other towns around there as well. It was so Pauper continued his lovely work and so he was getting a large sum of money every day.

Although Pauper was getting money from the sales of his work, his destiny of poverty and wretchedness did not let him know how the money vanished. He could not even buy cheap dresses but he was wearing the dirty rags all days as when he was in his Laketu town. And the worst of it was, his destiny was so powerful that he could not buy sufficient food to eat as much as he wanted to.

As Pauper got much honour and respect for his work it was just so Slanderer got honour and respect in respect of the right and wrong information which he was giving to the Ọba and chiefs. And in a few months' time, he had forgotten that he and Pauper were sojourners in Abalabi town. But he was behaving wickedly to the people as he wished.

# 12

## PAUPER AND SLANDERER COMPETE FOR
## A WIFE IN ABALABI TOWN

Thus Pauper, the Father of Wretchedness, continued his manner of living in poverty and wretchedness in this Abalabi town, while Slanderer continued his manner of living on wrong and right information given to the Ọba and his chiefs in this same town, until when a certain girl grew to the state of a maid. The maiden name of this maid was POPONDORO.

To put derision aside but to speak the truth, Creator who created Popondoro, wilfully created her with a such extraordinary beauty of which we cannot see the like or which does not exist under this sun these present days. And moreover, Creator who wilfully lavished this type of the strange beauty on Popondoro, needs to be glorified and honoured greatly.

After a little while, when Popondoro grew up further, Creator changed her beauty suddenly in a queer way to that of a mesmerism which was greater than the knowledge of a human being. This her kind of beauty was attracting people with full force like the magnet which attracts another iron forcibly.

As Popondoro's 'beauty of magnet' was so powerful, it was attracting young and old men and women of the town. Once one opened his or her eyes and looked at Popondoro, the strange damsel, there was no doubt her strange 'beauty of magnet' would draw that person with so much force that he or she would not be able to take his or her eyes away from Popondoro, the strange lass, until after she went away from that place.

For this her strange 'beauty of magnet' had much power of attracting people. Nearly all of the young men of Abalabi town were in the war to win the love of Popondoro, the wonderful maid, upon whom Creator had gracefully bestowed the magnificent 'beauty of magnet'.

Furthermore, nearly the whole of the young men of the town were saying greedily all about in the town that: 'But if Popondoro, the strange maid of maids, refuses to marry me, I shall commit suicide!' Every young man was shouting in great earnest.

But as time went on, and in particular all the young men of the town had now ceased to go and work on their farms. Instead of that every one of them was just following Popondoro, the possessor of 'beauty of magnet', about. Several parents of those young men, who understood the risk of such strange beauty as that of Popondoro and who were very civil, began to lock up their young sons in the rooms so that they might be free from the trap of maiden Popondoro's 'beauty of magnet'. The parents did so because 'the elders say that he who does not wish to be injured on the eyes by a sharp stick, must keep himself away before it reaches him'.

Well, among the countless young men who were struggling hard to gain the golden love of lass Popondoro, were Slanderer and Pauper. But Pauper and Slanderer were sojourners in Abalabi town and both were also close friends from their native town, Laketu.

But of course Brawler, whose brawls were just like 'outbreak of fire which makes one run', in her brawls did not forget Pauper, her husband. But she was still going about looking for him, although the strange pompous beauty of this damsel had forced Pauper to forget Brawler entirely.

But Slanderer had started immediately to find one way or the other to put Pauper in serious trouble from the day that he knew that he was one of those who were struggling to win the love of Popondoro. Slanderer was doing so because he knew well that Pauper was a very strong man but that he himself was a great sloth. But of course 'a hard-working man is the enemy of a lazy man'.

As the days went on the terrible war to win the golden love of Popondoro, the possessor of 'beauty of magnet', was becoming more tense among the young men. When the Ọba, chiefs and elders noticed this and were sure that famine was imminent to invade the town, then they summoned an emergency meeting immediately onto the assembly ground, in front of the Ọba's palace. At this meeting, father and mother of expensive Popondoro, were present.

'Well, you all chiefs, the elders and the Ọba who is the ruler of earth and who is second to the gods, and you all the rest of the people!' One chief stood up and first addressed the gathering. 'You are welcome.'

'The cause of summoning this emergency meeting is to let us sit and discuss together about the action that we should take to discourage the young men of the town from Popondoro's strange "beauty of magnet" which came miraculously on her a few months ago!' Another one of the chiefs made the object of the emergency meeting known to the gathering.

'Yes, you are correct. We must find the resolution which will stop the young men from following maiden Popondoro about, and which forced them to abandon their farms!' one of the elders suggested in earnest.

'And as the young men have abandoned their farms, surely, a serious famine will soon invade the town!' another chief supported the first chief in earnest.

'But I suggest a motion on what we should do to stop this on-coming famine, that we take Popondoro away from the town at once and hide her in one of our neighbouring towns. But then, when her wooers or suitors do not see her any more, all will go back to their farms!' another one of the elders moved this motion with restlessness of mind.

'Thank you very much. To take Popondoro away from the town is the only thing which will lessen the trouble in the town!' All of the chiefs and elders jointly approved that advice.

'But beware, you all chiefs and elders! If you take our daughter, Popondoro, away from this town which is her native town, this means, in fact, you deprive her of her right! For this reason, we are opposed to all of your proposals!' Popondoro's father and mother protested glumly.

'All right, it is not bad if you are opposed to all of our proposals. My own proposal is that it is very necessary to find a sort of drastic solution which will minimize her suitors and avoid bloodshed among them. Unless we examine every one of them very carefully and know his character, then we should choose one whose character is the best to marry Popondoro!' the Ọba who spoke last, brought this advice.

'Yes! This advice is the best of all!' the gathering of the chiefs, elders, Popondoro's father and mother shouted in joy, and then they adopted the Ọba's advice immediately.

But having adopted the Ọba's advice, the chiefs and the Ọba gave order to the elders to examine the character of every one of Popondoro's suitors. They told them to bring the name of the suitor whose character was the best to them in a short time. Then the Ọba brought the meeting to an end and then everyone returned to his or her house, expecting the result of the investigation.

But then the elders started their assignment at once. When they had examined the suitors for several days without sleeping and resting, they found two men whose characters seemed the best and who were eligible to marry Popondoro, whose strange 'beauty of magnet' was attracting people with full force.

The first man who was eligible was Slanderer, who was a close friend of Pauper. The second man was Pauper. The reason for selecting Slanderer was that he had wicked cunnings and was giving unfounded rumours to the Ọba and his chiefs, though he was lazy.

The reason for choosing the second man, Pauper, was that he was a very perfect wood-carver. Even the people of the town, the Ọba, the chiefs and the elders greatly admired the statue of the Ọba which he carved from the wood. The statue resembled the Ọba so much that the people and thousands of people of the other towns were rushing to the Aafin to see the statue with their eyes.

But it was a great pity that, in fact, Pauper was as strong as a buffalo and that he was number one wood-carver in Abalabi town, yet his destiny of poverty and wretchedness did not let money remain in his hands so long but he was wearing the same dirty rags about all days. Yet, Pauper would not believe that destiny existed.

It was like that the elders selected two men as those who were eligible to marry Popondoro, instead of one man among all of the young men who were struggling hard to win her love.

In the long run, when the result of the selection was out, the other suitors who were not selected and who were more than three thousand, started to grumble about in the town. Soon after, serious troubles started all over the town unexpectedly. The people of the town divided into three parts.

The people of the first part supported and followed Slanderer. Even though he was a sojourner in Abalabi town, he was the one who created the troubles with his wicked cunnings, particularly in respect of Pauper of whom he was a close friend.

The people of the second part backed and followed Pauper who was also a sojourner in this town.

Meanwhile the people of the third part protested, saying they did not welcome the selection, especially the way that the elders made it. They added to their protest that all they wanted was that the elders should make a kind of competition for the whole of Popondoro's suitors. The people of this same third part told the elders that they should remove Slanderer and Pauper out of the race. They said that they did not want sojourners to take part in the competition. But of course, the elders refused to take Slanderer and Pauper away from the competition. They told them that though they were sojourners, they were eligible to do such a thing as this one with the sons of the soil.

A few days later Slanderer started to put the oil into the fire of the scuffle with his wicked cunnings. The scuffle became so serious that Popondoro's suitors began to kill one another. And as time went on the suitors were dying in masses every day.

But in this great disaster, again, Slanderer began to cause riot all over the town. He 'shot the bow into the sky and then he covered himself with a mortar'. The people of the town and even the domestic animals were so confused that they did not know which was which this time.

54

When this disaster continued to spread on and on, the elders and chiefs did not waste time but they started to try their best to restore peace and order in the town. They were holding meetings both day and night, yet all their efforts failed.

In the end, they saw that their power could not stop this disaster, which Slanderer turned later to civil war, whether they liked it or not. They agreed to design a kind of very tough competition for all Popondoro's suitors.

At their meeting, the elder made a law which entitled the winner of the competition to marry Popondoro, the possessor of 'beauty of magnet'.

But then, a few days later, the elders invited the suitors to the assembly ground, in front of the palace. Having seen that all of them sat and were rapt but fastened their eyes on them, then the elders' Herald announced to the suitors that: 'Just to stop the bloodshed and killings and scuffle which have started in the town for the past few days, and having examined the situation of the town and of the people as a whole, we saw that the town and the innocent people would be ruined in a short time. But then we the elders, the chiefs and the Ọba agreed to make a competition for you as you have requested us to do!'

The Herald continued, he said: 'But the drastic competition is to make heaps on the field which we have already provided. And each of you will make twenty-one heaps. But any one of you who finishes his own first will be the winner and then he will marry Popondoro, the damsel!'

The Herald went on, he said: 'My advice is that every one of you should prepare himself ready with his hoe and cutlass, because the competition will take place in the morning of seven days to come! Do you all agree to make the competition of heaps or not?' Thus the Herald for the chiefs, the Ọba and elders announced to the suitors.

'We all agree to make the competition with happiness!' maiden Popondoro's suitors shouted at one time with great joy and contentment. Then the Herald brought the meeting to an end. And the suitors returned to their houses with laughter.

But it was as from that day every one of the suitors started to prepare himself ready for this tough wife competition, except Slanderer, who was a sloth among of the rest. He did not bother to prepare himself ready for he did not like a competition, because he was very sure that he would not be able to make even five heaps when his rivals would finish their own.

But of course, 'the shelf is just telling a lie, the loads belong to the ceiling'. Slanderer is not strong enough to win this sort of competition at all. Even if 'a dog wears the garment of fire, tiger the apron of blood and cat wraps its buttocks with rags, they are all in the same line with the carnivorous animals'. But Slanderer was one of thieves, sloths, tale-bearers and murderers. He was not tough enough to compete with Pauper, the man who was three-in-one.

However Slanderer might cause confusion and scuffle in the town, in the end, all his efforts would be in vain, unless he won this competition he would not be eligible to marry Popondoro.

Although, on the other hand, it was perfectly sure that Slanderer was so lazy that it was impossible for him to win the competition as 'danger is on the farm of "Longe" and "Longe" himself is a danger', so Slanderer was a danger entirely.

For instance, Slanderer with the help of his wicked cunnings, knew a powerful spell-man. After he had got a large sum of money from Slanderer, he prepared one powerful amulet for him before the day of the competition arrived. The work of the amulet was that when one spoke to it to do something, it would do it immediately. So Slanderer kept this amulet in his room.

After, he bought one cutlass which was a little bigger than a table-knife, then one hoe which was as small as a ladle. He kept them in his room as well. That was how Slanderer prepared himself ready for the tough wife competition.

But Pauper, the Father of Wretchedness, and the rest of the suitors put their hope on their hoes, cutlasses and their power, while Slanderer put his hope on his amulet and cunnings.

56

# 13

# THE DAY OF THE WIFE COMPETITION ARRIVES

When the day of the wife competition arrived, it was hardly daybreak when the whole of the competitors came and gathered in front of the Aafin or palace. Everyone held his hoe and cutlass. Then they were expecting the elders and chiefs to arrive.

But soon, little children, young and old, women and men, came and they stood round the suitor competitors in several circles. But then all of them began to mock at Slanderer continuously till when the chiefs and elders arrived. And they sat impressively in their seats, according to the title which each of them held in the office. Then they were expecting the father, mother and Popondoro to arrive.

A little after, father, mother and beautiful Popondoro, in her gorgeous dresses, arrived with their well-wishers, singers, drummers and minstrels.

Popondoro's father and mother sat in special carved seats. Popondoro sat amidst her father and mother. Their well-wishers sat on their left and right while the drummers, singers and minstrels who did not sit continued their amusements and dance.

Haa! That big morning, Popondoro, the damsel of damsels, beautified her delicate body much with the multifarious, gorgeous dresses that the glory of her 'beauty of magnet' increased to what could not be described simply by human beings.

And this glory of her beauty was such that thousands of people forced themselves into the circles of people with kick and fist in order to see Popondoro with their eyes on her beauty and enjoy her strange beautiful dresses, even if for only one minute before the chiefs and elders took her onto the proposed field of competition.

As lady Popondoro's 'beauty of magnet' forced uncountable spectators with its power of attraction to move here and there without their wish, just so it was forcing her suitors who were in a single line with their hoes and cutlasses in their hands to move heavily here and there. The beauty of her dresses and of herself began to intoxicate the whole people like hot drinks.

Not only this, but as her suitors forced themselves to stand stiffly on the line like the soldiers, and as they were looking at Popondoro with half an eye, soon the powerful magnet of her beauty began to attract them so much that they were unable to stand still at this time any more. But it forced them to stagger bit by bit towards the beautiful spot on which she sat amidst her father and mother.

'Haaa! Even if Popondoro can be my wife just for only one day! How happy will I be on earth!' one of Popondoro's suitors greedily yelled, suddenly.

'Haaa! But let glory and honour be to Creator who has lavished this kind of great "beauty of magnet" on Popondoro!' The spectators and other people were not aware when they began to shout in great earnest, at intervals to Popondoro.

'Ṣiọ! Look at this nuisance, an habitual tale-bearer, a sluggard and a rogue! He is holding the hoe and cutlass of poverty and he wants to marry Popondoro, the possessor of "beauty of magnet"! "We call a dog but the goat comes out". You foolish evil man who wants to marry Popondoro! Better you bolt away from this place now! Because "the elephant's head is not a load which a child can carry".' It was thus the spectators and other people derided and browbeat Slanderer that morning.

'Hun-un! You are stupid indeed; like the bird called "Ṣọ" which cries once in a year! Even if I am the most backward among us the suitors of Popondoro, I'm sure that I'm just like "a leper who cannot extract milk but can overturn it".' Slanderer gnashed and he explained in anger to the people. 'And further,' Slanderer went on, 'I know that I'm lazy more than the rest of Popondoro's suitors!' Slanderer continued to disclose to the people, he said:

'But surely, "I have a junior brother who is stronger than me",'
Slanderer explained to the people in indirect word.

But then as soon as Slanderer had told the people and the
spectators like that, he was about to tell the ground to split and
enter into it when the whole of the people, etc. snubbed him
from head to feet. But of course, the spectators and others did
not understand that Slanderer was just pointing out to them
that even if he was a sluggard, he had bought a powerful magic
amulet which he would use for the competition.

The spectators and others still continued to despise him
though shame had depressed him now. The chiefs arrived in
their beautiful and costly dresses. And as soon as they had
seated, their Herald announced to the crowd of people, he said:
'Now, let all people listen to me! It is this morning that
Popondoro's suitors will go and do their competition on the
proposed field! So it is time now to move onto the field!'

But then the Ọba's Ikọ carried the chairs and then they started
to go to the field.

So all Popondoro's suitors, elders, chiefs, Popondoro's father,
mother, herself, the drummers, singers, minstrels, well-wishers
and uncountable spectators started to jump high up and dance
in great joy along the way to the field of the competition.

The Ọba's Ikọ set the chairs in rows as soon as all had danced
merrily to the field. Popondoro's father and mother sat in the
chairs which were on the first row. Popondoro, in her gorgeous
dresses, sat between her father and mother, while their well-
wishers sat on their left and right.

The chiefs sat on the chairs of the second row, all elders sat on
the third row, nobles on the fourth row, while the spectators or
crowd of people sat on the chairs of the fifth row, which were
behind the rest.

As soon as the people had seated themselves comfortably
they were anxious to see the competitors in action, the Herald
led them to the second end of the field. He set them abreast in a
row, facing the people or gathering on the first end of the field.

Having done so, he returned to the first end. But as he
continued his arrangement, the morning sun appeared sud-

denly from the east of this field of competition, with its golden rays.

After the Herald had finished and was satisfied, and the gathering of people saw plainly that there was no partiality in his arrangement, then he returned to the competitors and he shouted: 'Now, let all of you get ready!' As he commanded, every one of them held his hoe ready for action. After, he shouted to them again: 'Let you bend down with your hoes in hands!' When they responded to his command, he shouted again: 'Start to make your heaps towards the gathering of people who are facing you!'

But then when they started their heaps, he returned to the people, he sat on a chair and there he kept watching them.

To everyone's surprise, as soon as the sun had shone from the east, a strange peaceful breeze started to blow onto the gathering of people just as if it knew what was happening on the field that day. And all at a sudden, the golden rays of the sun formed a strange beautiful crown on Popondoro's head. The people including Popondoro's father and mother were greatly alarmed and squirmed when they saw the beauty which the crown of the sun-rays added to Popondoro's 'beauty of magnet' unexpectedly at this time.

The gathering was still wondering about the crown when thousands of various kinds of small birds, with golden, silverish and bluish feathers, appeared suddenly. Then they started to perch on top of one tree and another. And their cries were a very lovely song which was so melodious that the people were not aware when they began to dance merrily in their seats. It was just as if these small beautiful birds were invited to this field of competition to add more to the joy of Popondoro's marriage.

The people were still dancing in their seats when another interesting thing happened again suddenly. This very time, uncountable insects flew onto the field. They were various kinds with their colours which attracted people indeed. Then they began to fly in swarms and slowly round the field as they were humming in different lovely tones. And their hums were a sort of revival for the competitors.

So also the beautiful slender trees which surrounded the field

60

with their attractive leaves were bowing to and fro in a slow motion and they were regarding Popondoro's 'beauty of magnet'. Just the same the green leaves which were on their branches were blowing merrily here and there, and were showing to the people that they were greeting Popondoro's happy marriage.

But those mighty trees seemed they were not so happy in respect of Pauper, who was one of the competitors. Those trees were not so happy because he used to fell them and after he used to carve them into different kinds of articles.

Hardly two minutes after the suitor competitors had started their heaps, they were covered with a cloud of dust like the smoke of a burning house. But there was none of them who bothered about that.

In 'a wink of monkey', Pauper, the thoughtless strong man, the ragged man and the man of men, had outrun his rivals, when Slanderer, the man who had in him the whole of the wicked characters of earth, was the most behind all.

But when Popondoro saw Pauper in front of the others, she began to sing a fascinating song with such a strange voice and in joy which could not be described. And again, she was flattering him. But when Pauper was much encouraged by Popondoro's lovely song and flattery, he became nearly mad at once. His power became tripled immediately.

Meanwhile, as soon as the rest of the suitor competitors heard Popondoro's song and flattery, they became so dejected that many of them fainted and fell down. The cause of their fainting was that it seemed to them now that it was likely to be Pauper who Popondoro took to be her most favourite, but they were not yet very sure of that.

Now, having seen this and that he was the only one who was far behind the rest, Slanderer brought his magic amulet from his pocket. Having touched his tongue with it, he commanded loudly: 'Pauper! Pauper! Pauper! Whatever we tell "Ọgbọ" to do that "Ọgbọ" does! Whatever we tell "Ọgba" to do that "Ọgba" does! But my magic amulet, let the handle of Pauper's hoe break now!'

61

But all the elders, chiefs, nobles, crowd of spectators, Popondoro's father, mother, their well-wishers and Popondoro herself were shocked in fear and they wondered greatly when they saw that Slanderer had hardly commanded his magic amulet when the handle of Pauper's hoe broke into two.

The whole of them shook their heads suddenly and were sulky at Slanderer for his evil deed. Even Popondoro was so much perplexed that she nearly fainted. But Slanderer was greatly shamed when the people despised him greedily.

But as soon as Pauper shouted to Slanderer in proverb and in bravery that: 'But the shelf is just telling a lie, the loads belong to the ceiling', then he took his cutlass, he ran into the nearby forest. He felled one big tree. But as his profession was wood-carving, within five minutes, he carved a new handle of hoe from that tree. Pauper did not waste time at all, 'in a wink of crab', he ran back onto the field, although his rivals including Slanderer had made their heaps farther than where he had reached before his hoe was broken.

But then he continued his own heaps and 'in a wink of monkey' he overtook his suitor rivals and 'in a wink of crab' he outran them by two heaps.

Now, Pauper, the powerful man like the buffalo, the rag-wearer, was in front of all again. But when Popondoro, whose 'beauty of magnet' had such power to attract people, her father, mother and the other people saw how Pauper was making his heaps with all his power towards them, all began to clap loudly for him and all were shouting to him cheerfully, that: 'Pauper, put more efforts! Put more power! Gee up and become the husband of Popondoro today!'

And moreover, this time, Popondoro modulated her song to that of a more encouraging one, which gave more power to Pauper immediately he listened to it. So this song made it clear now to the other wife competitors that Popondoro had chosen Pauper to be her most favourite. Now, Slanderer, in great anger, commanded his magic amulet as usual to break the handle of Pauper's hoe and it broke into two at once.

Though Pauper was as strong as a giant and was leading in the competition, depression overwhelmed him so much at this time that he stood upright lazily. He supported his buttocks lazily and then he forgot himself, standing on the same spot like a dead man.

But when Popondoro saw that Pauper was so depressed this time that he could not go further in his heaps, with her golden voice, she started to sing the song of revival for him. But as soon as the song aroused him he took his cutlass and the broken handle of his hoe. Then he ran into the forest.

Pauper hastily felled one 'idin' tree and 'in a wink of monkey' he carved a new handle of hoe from it. As he was carving the handle it was so he was stretching out his neck just to see how far his suitor rivals had gone in their heaps.

As soon as he had finished the handle and when he wanted to run back onto the field, it was this very moment that a feeble old woman stood up suddenly in the green forest which was near there. She was not so far from the place at which Pauper carved the new handle of his hoe. But he did not see this feeble old woman all the time that he was carving the handle.

This feeble old woman began to wave her hands to Pauper and she was shouting to him with her hoarse voice, saying: 'Please, I beg you, come and help me put my load onto my head! Please, help me!'

'Haaa! Old mother, don't disturb me! Please, forgive me!' Pauper shouted hurriedly and in earnest.

'Haa, what are you hurrying for, my son?' the old woman pleaded further. 'There is nothing on earth which is better than to help the old people! Remember now that, "the hand of a child cannot reach the top of a shelf and so that of an old person cannot enter into the calabash!" A child should not refuse when he is sent on an errand by an old person!' the feeble old woman reminded Pauper with her hoarse voice.

But when this old woman appealed to Pauper like that and being merciful and a humble young man since when he was a boy, although his destiny of poverty and wretchedness were torturing him much, then as he held his new handle of hoe, he ran to this feeble old woman. In a hurry, he shouted to her: 'Old

63

mother, bend down, bend down and let me put your load onto your head!' But as Pauper was hurrying to the old woman it was so he was stretching out his neck many times just to see how far his rivals had gone in their heaps.

'But what are you hurrying like this for, my son?' the old woman asked instead of bending down and letting Pauper put her load onto her head in time.

'Hooo! I am competing for a wife, but if I win, one damsel whose name is Popondoro will be my wife today! But there is one man among us who is also a competitor and he is so greedy that he breaks the handle of my hoe with his magic amulet each time that I am in front of all others. But he does this evil deed so that he may win the beautiful lady!' Pauper explained in a hurry.

'Is that your problem? Well, it isn't bad yet! "One who is not a clothing embroiderer wears embroidered clothes but how much more for the embroiderer himself." Your hoe will not break again, my son! But just stretch your new handle of hoe nearly to touch my nostrils!' The old woman wanted to help Pauper in a miraculous way.

When Pauper stretched the new handle of his hoe so that it nearly touched the old woman's nostrils, she blew out mucus from her nose onto the handle. Having done that, she told him that each time Slanderer commanded his magic amulet to break the handle of his hoe, he should shout in haste that: 'It is forbidden! An old woman's mucus never cut while the handle of the hoe which is carved from "idin" tree never break!'

When the feeble old woman had taught Pauper the incantation which would repress the power of Slanderer's magic amulet, she bent down, the Pauper put her load onto her head and soon, she went away.

But then, 'in a wink of monkey' Pauper ran back onto the field of the competition. He continued his heaps at once. Even if his suitor rivals, including Slanderer, had made their heaps far from where he had reached before his hoe broke, 'in a wink of crab' he overtook them and 'in a wink of monkey' he outran them by six heaps.

Now, this tough competition was nearing its end, and Pauper was in front of the rest. Meanwhile, it was sure that he would be the winner. But when Slanderer saw now that there was no doubt Pauper was going to win, he commanded his usual magic amulet to break the handle of Pauper's hoe. But Pauper hastily shouted that: 'The shelf is just telling a lie, the loads belong to the ceiling'. After, he recited aloud the incantation which the feeble old woman taught him. He said: 'It is forbidden, old woman's mucus never break and so the handle which is carved from "idin" tree never break!' So Pauper's handle of his hoe did not break this time.

'But why Pauper's handle of hoe does not break this time? Has he got something whose power has repressed my magic amulet?' Slanderer shook his head to left and right and retorted painfully. 'All right,' Slanderer continued, he said: 'I shall wait and see whether Pauper will be the winner of Popondoro. But if Popondoro will not be for me in the end, she will not be for Pauper as well!' he said earnestly.

'In fact, "termites are trying, but they cannot chew the stone", that is forbidden,' Slanderer retorted further within himself. 'But "if it is not possible for the rat to eat the sese beans it will scatter them uselessly instead",' Slanderer lamented angrily.

'O well! But with all my wicked cunnings,' Slanderer shook his head in earnest and then he went further, 'I shall find one way or the other to disturb Pauper from marrying Popondoro!'

He continued his evil plan, he said: 'I am sure of myself that I'm just like "a leper who cannot extract milk but can overturn it".' It was like that Slanderer stood on one spot, supporting his buttocks, and then he began to plan his evil deed within himself how he would disturb Pauper from marrying Popondoro if he himself failed to marry her.

Inasmuch as Slanderer was still in confusion at the failure in the end of his magic amulet, on the power of which he depended to win the wife competition. Pauper had made his heaps very far so that there were only two heaps which remained for him to make and win Popondoro. But then when Slanderer was sure that Pauper was already the winner, he threw his hoe and cutlass upon the ground. Then with his evil cunnings, he started to walk zigzag along to Popondoro who sat amidst her father and mother, in her strange 'beauty of magnet' and 'the crown of rays of sun' on her head.

When there remained just a short distance to reach her, he rushed furiously against her in great anger. He grasped her unexpectedly. But when he wanted to run away with her, Popondoro's father, mother, the chiefs, the elders and the crowd of spectators started to struggle to take her back from him.

But as soon as Pauper saw that Slanderer wanted to steal her away, he ran to her and then he joined hands with the other people. But all were still struggling to take her back from Slanderer, when the rest of the competitors threw their hoes and cutlasses away. In anger, all ran to Popondoro. Then every one of them started to struggle to take her and run away with her.

After all, however, as 'the truth never strays, but lying wanders into the bush', Popondoro's father, mother and the rest of the people, including Pauper, struggled so hard that in the long run they overpowered Slanderer and the other suitor competitors, and they took Popondoro back from them. And without hesitation, they gave her to Pauper who won the competition. Now, Popondoro, who was beautified with 'beauty of magnet' by Creator, became Pauper's wife in the end.

But as soon as Popondoro's father and mother released her to Pauper, he put her on his shoulder. But as he held his cutlass firmly, he began to run along into the forest in which there was an enormous and very tall tree. And he had run far with Popondoro before the other hostile suitor competitors saw him. Having seen Popondoro on his shoulder, with the 'crown of rays of sun' on her head, all of them started to chase him in order to take the damsel from him.

But as Pauper was a wood-carver and that he had the art of climbing tall trees, this helped him so much that 'in a wink of crab' he had carried Popondoro onto the topmost of that enormous tree before the rest of the competitors came. Then he hid her inside a huge hole which was on the topmost of that tree.

When he was sure that Popondoro was quite safe, then he held his cutlass firmly and he descended gently from the tree. But his feet had hardly touched the ground when the rest of the competitors, including Slanderer, rushed against him. They were beating him mercilessly. But as he was as strong as a giant, he began to beat them mercilessly in return.

It was like that they continued to beat one another from that tree until they reached the town. But as they were still beating one another in the town, the Ọba ordered his guides to go and arrest them and bring them before him.

He found those who had failed the competition guilty of breach of peace. But he warned them that they must not fight with Pauper any longer. He confirmed to them that Pauper was the winner of the competition. Therefore, he was the rightful man to marry Popondoro, though Pauper was alien in Abalabi town.

Having warned them seriously to keep peace and order in the town, then every one of them hastily 'put his child's hands into his clothes' and then he went quietly to his house. It was like that the suitor competition came to a hostile scuffle in the end.

# 14

# BRAWLER MEETS PAUPER AT THE
# MARRIAGE CEREMONY OF HIS NEW WIFE

Well, when it was evening, Pauper went back to the tree. He climbed it and he brought Popondoro down. Although there was dark at that time, the 'crown of the brilliant rays of sun' which was made to adorn Popondoro's head by Creator, helped Pauper and Popondoro so much that they saw the road through to the town.

But as 'what one likes most is what will form the greater part of his possessions; the owner of two hundred slaves dies but is found to have only one garment', so it was true that in the end, Pauper won Popondoro. But it was a pity indeed that as he was making a lot of money on his wood-carving, he had not more than the same dirty rags which were on his body since when he had been driven away from his Laketu town. And all of his friends did not know how his money was vanishing without reason.

But it was now they understood that his destiny of poverty and wretchedness were punishing him indeed. But alas, Pauper had not yet agreed even slightly till now that there was something which was called destiny.

But after a few days and when there was peace all over the town, the chiefs and the Ọba made an important meeting. Their main discussion in the meeting was about Slanderer's evil cunnings with which he caused confusion, scuffle and great disaster in the town in which many people died, in order to win the love of Popondoro. For his evil character, the Ọba gave order to his chiefs and the elders to expel him out of Abalabi town.

It was like that Slanderer left the town with great shame just as he was expelled out of his native town, Laketu.

When there remained three days before Pauper was going to perform the marriage ceremony of his new wife, and in order not to be a great shame for him, his friends lent him one huge embroidered pair of trousers, one large embroidered garment and one embroidered cap with flaps. All of these special dresses were mainly for this sort of ceremony.

In addition, they bought one big fat ram and all ingredients of the soup, and many other kinds of eatable things with which to eat the ram. They bought several kegs of palm wine as well.

The ram was slaughtered on the day of the ceremony and the house-women cooked all and then they brought all to the front of the house. The palm wine was brought to the outside as well.

Then a few minutes later, the drummers arrived and they started to beat their drums immediately. But as Pauper, in borrowed dresses, his friends and many other well-wishers were eating, it was so they were drinking and dancing merrily.

But as this marriage ceremony was great, it attracted nearly one thousand spectators at once. All surrounded the circle of the dance, in front of the house in which Pauper, the bridegroom, was living.

Now, I bring it to the memory again that some years ago, the Ọba of Laketu town, who was Pauper's father, with his chiefs expelled Pauper, in respect of his overmuch poverty and wretchedness, Brawler, in respect of her continuous and harmful brawls, and Slanderer, in respect of his wicked behaviours. But that day the Ọba cursed as well upon Pauper and Brawler, his wife, that wherever Pauper was, Brawler would be there with him, and that wherever Brawler was, Pauper would be there with her.

Furthermore, we should not forget that it was with brawls and in anger that Brawler chased Pauper from Laketu town until they were near one crossroads at which several feeder-roads met. But as Pauper was faster that day, he had run to that crossroads but then he had run to the road which went to the westward. But when Brawler ran to that same crossroads, she mistakenly took the road which went to the eastward. She thought that was the right road which her husband took. It was like that both of them missed each other that day.

When Pauper was travelling along this westward road as fast as he could, Slanderer ran and later he overtook him. But then both of them continued to travel along till when they came to this town called Abalabi. But it was just the same for Brawler. She travelled on and on, on that wrong road till when she came to a town called Ṣodeji.

But Brawler did not stay so long at Ṣodeji town, the people of that town drove her away from there when her brawls did not let them have the rest of minds.

But when she left there she continued to look about for her husband till she came to Abalabi town in which her husband and Slanderer had been sojourning for a long time. But she was not aware that her husband and Slanderer were in this town, because it was a big town indeed.

But being 'joy has a transient body', is that as Pauper and his friends were eating and drinking in great joy, and as the drummers were flattering Pauper with their drums 'in nines and tens', and his great showy character in his borrowed embroidered dresses was strange, the crowd of spectators began to shout loudly at him so much that their shouts filled the sky.

But when Brawler heard the continuous shouts, without hesitation, and with her hot brawls, she started to come to the place of the marriage ceremony, just to see what was happening there. But she did not know that it was Pauper, her husband, who was performing the marriage ceremony of his new wife, Popondoro, whose 'beauty of magnet' was above the knowledge of mankind.

When Brawler arrived at the circle of the dance and when she looked round the circle of the dance, she saw her husband, in very costly borrowed embroidered dresses and he was dancing merrily. But of course, 'a drunkard forgets poverty when he is drinking'. It was a pity that Pauper had forgotten his poverty and wretchedness entirely at this moment of his merriment.

'Haaa! Pauper, are you this? My hands catch you today!' But

when Brawler shouted harshly to Pauper like that and Pauper raised his head up and saw her, fear overwhelmed him so much that he began to shiver immediately. And in shivering, he ran like lightning into the room in which Popondoro sat in the glory of her beauty. 'In a wink of monkey', Brawler too, ran like lightning into that room.

But the spectators were confused by what was happening now to Pauper, and it was so this sudden happening confused Pauper's friends. All of them just guessed that Pauper had become insane suddenly by the transient joy of his new wife, Popondoro. Without wasting much time, they ran into the room just to be sure of what had forced Pauper to run into the room.

But they were afraid indeed when they met Pauper, packing all his rags in haste, and prepared to run away. And it was just the same for Popondoro. She did not understand what had happened unexpectedly to Pauper so much like that, so that he started to pack his rags in fear and haste.

But of course, when he explained to his friends in haste and in unrest of mind that Brawler was his wife, and they saw that she was biting him repeatedly like a dog, and he was preparing to flee with the costly embroidered dresses which they lent to him, without hesitation, they removed the dresses away from his body. But Pauper had hardly worn his dirty rags again when his wife, Brawler drove him fiercely to the outside. And it was so his friends and Popondoro, his new wife, in her glory of 'beauty of magnet', ran in great fear and confusion to the outside.

Immediately the spectators saw that Pauper, his friends and Popondoro ran to the outside in fear and confusion. They scattered suddenly in confusion. Everyone took to his or her heels. So this horrible happening became the matter of 'if you cannot run, leave the way for me'. The drummers were so fearful and confused that they hardly waited and took their drums along with them when they were running for their lives.

But as soon as the whole people had escaped from the circle of the dance, Brawler started to chase Pauper along fiercely in his usual dirty rags like a madman.

71

It was so Brawler continued to chase and bite Pauper away from this Abalabi town, as the people yelled at him and derided him in laughter.

Thus Pauper's destiny forced him to lose Popondoro, whose strange beauty used to attract people by force like a strong magnet. But it was a great pity that Pauper had not yet believed till now that destiny existed, and that it was the unfortunate destiny which he chose from Creator when coming to earth that was the cause of all his misfortunes.

# 15

## PAUPER AND BRAWLER ARRIVE AT
## MỌKỌLỌKI TOWN

It was so Brawler continued to chase her husband, Pauper, fiercely from Abalabi town without stopping till she chased him to a town called Mọkọlọki at about five o'clock in the evening. But she was so tired that she could no longer bite her husband. The tiredness also caused illness to her.

When they ran helter-skelter into that town, they lodged at the house of the Baalẹ or the head of this town. This Baalẹ being kind and loving strangers much, he gave food to the couple. After, he started to treat Brawler for her illness immediately as well.

Truly, the Baalẹ was kind to Pauper and his wife according to how Creator had created him. But Pauper was not so happy for this because he was sure that when his wife was well, she would continue her harmful brawls. But then the Baalẹ and the people of the town would soon become fed up with her brawls.

Now, Pauper began to think within himself how he could run away from this Mọkọlọki town before the brawls of his wife were known to the people, because he knew well that 'it is sickness which can be cured but not death'. Brawler's brawls could not be cured. Unfortunately, he had no chance to run away till his wife was recovered from her illness. And truly, she was hardly well when she continued to brawl about inside the Baalẹ's house.

At the first instance, her brawls were greatly strange to the Baalẹ and his people. For them, her brawls were just like 'the fashion which has never existed'. But having looked at Brawler for a while in wonder and fear, the Baalẹ invited her husband into one of his rooms. First of all, he asked his name from him. But

Pauper replied that: 'My name is Pauper, the Father of Wretched-ness! But sometimes people call me Pauper!'

'What? Pauper, the Father of Wretchedness is your name?' the Baalẹ was shocked with fear and then he repeated the name.

'That is my name, Chief!' Pauper confirmed loudly.

'Is that so? All right!' But is there a quarrel between you and your wife or why is she brawling hotly like this?' the Baalẹ wondered.

'Not at all!' Pauper replied in shame and sadness.

'By the way, what is your wife's name?' asked the Baalẹ.

'Her name is Brawler!'

'Brawler or what?' the Baalẹ was greatly startled.

'Her name is Brawler!' Pauper confirmed in pensiveness.

'But I am afraid your wife's name and that of your own are shockers!' the Baalẹ remarked. 'But what is the name of your town?' the Baalẹ asked further.

'My town is called Laketu. The Ọba of Laketu town is my father. But the Ọba and his chiefs had changed Brawler, my wife, my close friend called Slanderer, and me to immortals. Then they expelled the three of us from the town!' Pauper explained in brief to the Baalẹ.

'Hun-un! But your explanations confuse my eyes indeed! Because the garment which you wear, your trousers and the cap on your head, all are dirty multi-rags like that of a madman. But you said you are a prince of Laketu town. But however a prince is poor and wretched, he will wear better dresses. And however it is bad for a prince, the royal blood will still remain in his body!' The Baalẹ was confused and wondered greatly.

'I have told you the truth, Baalẹ. I am the prince of the Ọba of Laketu town. But as I am much poor and wretched, then the Ọba drove me out of his palace!' Pauper explained further to the Baalẹ.

But then when the Baalẹ could no longer endure Brawler's painful brawls, he and Pauper left the room. They went to the front of the house. But as soon as they sat on the pavement and the Baalẹ just wanted to continue his questions, Brawler came to them again. She continued to brawl to and fro in front of them.

Soon, the Baalẹ's neighbours heard Brawler's brawls. Then they rushed out and gathered in front of the Baalẹ's house. They began to look at Brawler in amazement.

But the Baalẹ's neighbours were still fastening their eyes on Brawler when Slanderer came to the Baalẹ's house. He greeted the Baalẹ and he responded beautifully, not knowing that Slanderer had known the Baalẹ before. So he asked Slanderer to sit near him.

Now, as soon as Slanderer had seated he saw Pauper sitting closely to the Baalẹ. Then he greeted Pauper and he responded happily. Slanderer thought that Pauper would not accept his greetings in respect of the wife competition in which both of them took part in Abalabi town, when he used to break the handle of Pauper's hoe with his magic amulet in order to win the competition. But Pauper did not take Slanderer's evil deed seriously.

But when Slanderer told the Baalẹ that he lived at Ọfadafa'juro town, he asked him whether he would allow Pauper and his wife to follow him and live with him in that town. But with happiness, Slanderer agreed to take Pauper and his wife to that town so that the three of them might live together again.

But it was a pity indeed that Pauper did not think well before he agreed to follow Slanderer to Ọfadafa'juro town. He had forgotten that Slanderer was very cunning and that all his characters were evil.

However, when the Baalẹ stood up, he entered one room. A few minutes later, he brought out two pairs of trousers, two garments and two caps. Then he offered one pair of trousers, one garment and one cap to Pauper and so for Slanderer.

Then having given them nice food, but Brawler's hot brawls did not allow her to eat from the food, he bade them goodbye.

It was like that the Baalẹ or chief of Mọkọlọki town drove Pauper, Brawler and Slanderer away from his town with a trick because Brawler's brawls frightened him and his people indeed.

That was how Pauper and Slanderer united again.

# 16

## PAUPER, BRAWLER AND SLANDERER IN
## ỌFADAFA'JURO TOWN

It was about one-third through the day that Pauper, the Father of Wretchedness, Brawler and Slanderer left Mọkọlọki town and started their journey to the town called Ọfadafa'juro.

But as they were travelling along as fast as they could, after a while, Brawler's non-stop brawls harmed Slanderer and Pauper so much that instead of walking fast they started to wobble along the road now and in great depression. But of course, they were depressed, and after a while, Slanderer asked Pauper: 'Although you won Popondoro, you lost her in the end. But do you believe now that it is your bad destiny which had caused that to you?'

'No! No! I don't believe at all that destiny exists!' Pauper frowned at Slanderer.

'Well, as time goes on, you will see that destiny exists and that it causes your misfortune every time!' Slanderer said.

Late in the evening, however, they arrived at Ọfadafa'juro town and the three of them started to live together in one middle-aged man's house. But as 'one who travels far eats in a condemned mortar' is that at the time they came to this town, the food-stuffs were very scarce there. It was even very hard for them to get the lizard's yams to eat. Even Brawler ate the lizard's yams more than Slanderer and Pauper for she had nearly died of hunger.

When it was at night, they slept. But Slanderer and Pauper and the rest of the people in that house were woken suddenly in the morning by Brawler's harmful brawls. The people feared greatly when they were hearing the brawls. Because that was the first time in their lives that they experienced these sorts of brawls.

And it was as from that morning that Brawler showed them whom she was.

But as Pauper was as strong as a giant, though his destiny of misfortune was punishing him severely, it was hardly morning when he went to the blacksmith who made his carving tools for him.

In the morning of the third day that Pauper, Brawler and Slanderer had arrived in this town, Pauper took his carving tools. He went into the forest and he felled a big tree. Having carved it into several kinds of images and domestic utensils, he carried them to the town. But the people rushed anxiously to them and they bought all within a few minutes because they were very beautiful.

But as Pauper was an open-handed man, he, Brawler and Slanderer were using the money which he was realizing from his works for buying their food.

But what kind of work was it which Slanderer was doing whenever he woke up in the morning? He did nothing except to wobble about in the town. He told the women all over the town that he was a money-doubler and that he was able to double their money for them. But having heard this lie from Slanderer, the women gave their money to him, to double it for them. But as 'one who wants gain wants loss', is so Slanderer was not a money-doubler at all. But he lavished their money instead. But then they began to hate him.

In a short time, Pauper began to get rest of mind in this Ọfadafa'juro town. But his wife used to give him much problem every day, because she did nothing more than brawl about in the town every day. But soon, the people were so fed up with her brawls that in the end they took her to be the clad madwoman.

Inasmuch as Slanderer had deceived the women that he was a money-doubler and that he had taken a large sum of money from them, but he failed to double it for them and he did not refund their money to them. But as it is 'if the trap fails to catch a prey, it should return the bait', is that when Slanderer failed to refund their money, the women gathered together. They went to the Ọba and accused him of taking money from them by false pretence.

77

As soon as the Ọba had heard this from them, he gave the Staff of Order to one of his Ikọ or messengers, to go and arrest Slanderer with it. According to the custom of Ọfadafa'juro town. This Staff of Order was just like the warrant or summons paper still in existence. Slanderer was very fearful and he was half-conscious immediately the Staff was given to him. But as he held it and he was following the Ikọ along to the palace, Brawler followed them as she was brawling hotly. And the crowd of people who were making mockery of Slanderer, were following them to the Aafin or palace. But he was so ashamed that morning that he begged the ground to split and let him hide himself inside of it. But Brawler's brawls which she was brawling continuously along prevented her from shame.

But what was worse than anything was that when the Ọba's Ikọ brought Slanderer before the Ọba and his chiefs, and as the Ọba asked Slanderer whether it was true he had taken money from the women to everyone's surprise, without hesitation Brawler simply jumped suddenly to the front of the Ọba and his chiefs, instead of letting Slanderer defend himself, she began to brawl hotly.

When the Ọba and his chiefs were fed up with her brawls, the Ọba asked some of those people: 'By the way, from where did this madwoman come?' But those people explained to the Ọba that she lived in the same house in which Slanderer lived.

'What is her name?' the Ọba asked in astonishment.

'Her name is Brawler,' Slanderer hastily replied.

'Brawler or what?' the Ọba and his chiefs were greatly startled because it was strange to them to hear that the son of man bore this kind of name.

'Just so, Kabiyesi,' Slanderer replied.

'How long ago did she come to this town?'

'About three months ago,' Slanderer replied.

'Who is her husband?'

'Her husband is a close friend of mine and he is a wood-carver.'

'But what is his name?'

'His name is Pauper, the Father of Wretchedness, but some-

78

times we call him Pauper, Kabiyesi!' Slanderer explained to the Ọba.

'Pauper, the Father of Wretchedness, or what did you call his name?' the Ọba and his chiefs were shocked and they sat up in their seats. Then they looked at one another's eyes in shock when Slanderer confirmed to them that his name was Pauper, the Father of Wretchedness.

But it was very difficult for the Ọba and his chiefs to hear Slanderer's explanations. Because Brawler was brawling so hotly this time that her noises filled up the Aafin.

But after the Ọba fastened his eyes on Brawler for about five minutes without even a wink. He raised his head up again and he fastened it on the ceiling, thinking what he should do for these three strange persons, who were Pauper, Brawler and Slanderer. But when he dropped his head down, he gave the order to one of his Ikọ that he should expel them out of his town the following morning.

Fortunately, Brawler's brawls forced the Ọba to forget the accusation which the women made against Slanderer, that he took money from them by false pretence. When the Ọba said that he did not want Pauper, Brawler and Slanderer in his town, Brawler and Slanderer returned to the house.

But before they reached the house, Pauper had returned from the forest to the house before them. However, Slanderer told Pauper that the Ọba had given the order to his Ikọ to expel them from the town the following day. But Slanderer did not tell Pauper the truth of the causes of their banishment.

When Pauper heard this from Slanderer, in great sorrow, he lamented immediately that: 'Alas, but how could I avoid Brawler!' Pauper was despaired for he thought that it was Brawler alone who caused their banishment. He did not understand that Slanderer was the one who had particularly caused it and that Brawler was just a partaker.

But as soon as Pauper lamented about his wife, Brawler, Slanderer, with his usual wicked cunnings, told him that: 'Brawler's problem is a simple matter. But what we are going to do is that while Brawler is still sleeping, in the dead-night, we will pack our belongings. Then we will leave the town. But before she wakes in morning, we shall have travelled far away.' It was like that Slanderer told Pauper what they should do.

But then, according to Slanderer's evil plan, when it was the dead-night and when the hands and feet were at rest, Pauper and Slanderer packed their belongings. They left Brawler in her sleep but they went out cautiously.

Having travelled for three days, they came to one town called Abanirẹ. But it was not so long after they had started to live in this town that Slanderer, the sluggard, was wobbling about in this town. He heard from the people that there was a town which was surrounded by very rich lands. Slanderer learned as well that the town was at a distance of forty kilometres from Abanirẹ town.

But as Pauper was a hard-working man, he agreed to go and make a farm in that town, when Slanderer advised him. But as both of them could not stay so long in this Abanirẹ town, so they bought hoes, cutlasses and many other kinds of the farm implements. It was like that they prepared to move to another town where there were rich lands.

But we should not forget that Pauper and Slanderer had left Brawler in Ọfadafa'juro town while she was still fast asleep. But when she woke in the morning and did not see her husband and Slanderer, she understood at once that both of them had conspired together and fled from her.

But it was that very morning she left Ọfadafa'juro town and then she started to seek about for her husband.

# 17

# PAUPER AND SLANDERER GO AND FARM
# IN ARARỌMI TOWN

As soon as Slanderer and Pauper had bought their farm implements, they went direct to Ararọmi town where there were very rich lands.

Having got to the town, they were fortunate indeed. They found the fertile lands on the north and south parts of this town. But the lands on the east and west were barren entirely.

Of course, the lands to the north and south were deep and uncultivated since the beginning of the earth. Mighty trees were here and there in them and litters of decayed leaves filled up the ground.

So Pauper chose the rich land of the north. But the first important thing which he did was that he built one farmhouse near the rich forest. He was living in that house instead of living in the vicinity of the famous Ararọmi town as Slanderer did.

But as Pauper was as strong as a buffalo, he cleared the land without any problem. After, he made the heaps ready for the imminent rains of the year, so that he might plant maize and other kinds of crops with the first rain.

But as 'a lazy man chooses easy work to do', so Slanderer went to the east. He made his farm on the barren land instead of making it on the lands of the north or south, because he was too lazy to do hard work like Pauper. Then he made heaps on the barren land easily for there were no trees or any refuse.

When both friends had made their farms ready for the imminent rains, they started to pay visits to each other regularly, even if the north where Pauper made his farm was a bit far from the east.

It was not so long before the first rain of the year rained. But then Pauper planted his maize and the other kinds of crops on his rich land, while Slanderer planted his own on his barren land of the east.

Within three weeks that the rains had started to rain continuously, Pauper's maize shot out and thrived so well that each stalk was thick and the ears were growing very beautifully. And after less than two months, it was nearing its maturity.

But Slanderer's maize was not good at all. The stalks were yellow because he planted it on the barren land.

One day, Slanderer accompanied Pauper to his maize farm. But it was a great sorrow to him when he saw how well Pauper's maize thrived. He saw as well how each stalk was thick and the ears were green and the corn-cobs on each of the stalks were very robust.

But as 'a barren woman is jealous of a woman who has children and a lazy man is jealous of a hard-working man', so from the day that Slanderer had seen how well Pauper's maize had thrived, he started to behave to him like a friend and like an enemy. Slanderer had forgotten that Pauper had toiled hard before he made his farm on that rich land.

However, Slanderer returned to his house in the vicinity of Araromi town. In the evening, he sat in front of his house. But with his face distorted by grief, he became startled suddenly when he remembered Pauper's beautiful maize. And he was not aware when he shouted in greed: 'Haaa! Don't you see now how Pauper's maize has thrived well, is very green and bears robust corn-cobs? But look at my own how its stalks are thin while its ears are yellow and they bear not even one corn-cob! But what did I come to do at Araromi town then?'

Slanderer continued his sorrowful despair, he said: 'But of course "if the rat fails to eat the sese beans it will scatter them useless". But what I shall do is that I shall deceive Pauper so much that he will believe whatever I tell him.'

Slanderer went on in his evil plan, he said: 'I will tell a lie to Pauper that the Oba of Araromi town has made an order that all farmers in his land should cut their maize down or he would kill he who refused to comply with his order at once!'

Slanderer went further, he said: 'Haa! I, Slanderer, the great cunning man! I, the man on whom Creator has bestowed the evil cunnings of this earth! I, "the treacherous man who invites the thief to go and steal from the farm and then informs the owner of the farm to go and keep watch of his farm".'

Slanderer planned further: 'Surely, Pauper will believe my lie. Because he lives in his farmhouse so he cannot know what is going on in the town!' It was thus Slanderer planned how he would deceive Pauper to destroy his well-thrived maize.

'But Slanderer, why are you planning to destroy Pauper's maize?' a goodly man who overheard Slanderer's evil plan asked in earnest.

'Hee! You goodly man, better you keep to your own affair. But don't interfere with my plan. But is Pauper your relative?' Slanderer warned the man in anger.

'But, but, it is bad indeed to destroy our companion's or neighbour's property!' the goodly man advised Slanderer.

'But it is a simple thing for me to do an evil thing to my companions. And that is one of my choices from Creator. Do you understand me?' Slanderer frowned at the goodly man.

'Hun-un. Is that how you are? Well, of course, "the truth fails to sell in the market, but lies are bought with ready cash". Certainly, sooner or later, vengeance is coming upon the evil-doer, goodbye!' the goodly man told Slanderer, and then he went away at once.

But it was hardly the following morning when Slanderer took his cutlass. He went to his maize field and without hesitation, he cut the whole stalks of his maize down. Then the following morning, he went to Pauper in his farmhouse. He greeted him in a grievous voice. But Pauper responded jovially. After, he gave him a seat and he sat as false grief showed on his face. Then Pauper served him with nice food. Having finished with the food, he put one big keg of undiluted palm wine and one tumbler in front of him.

But immediately Slanderer had drunk the last drop of the palm wine, he covered his head suddenly with both his palms. Then he began to weep bitterly and sorrowfully. Slanderer wept so bitterly that Pauper was nearly crazy.

'But, Slanderer, what are you weeping like this for?' Pauper asked in a trembling voice.

'Huu, huu, huu!' Slanderer in his cunning did not tell Pauper what he was weeping for.

'Please, tell me, what are you weeping for?' Pauper asked again in great confusion.

'The Ọba's Ikọ! The Ọba's Ikọ! Huu, huu, huuu!' Slanderer continued his pretence but Pauper did not understand what he was telling him.

'But what did the Ọba and his Ikọ have done to you?' Pauper was so much perplexed that he did not know what he was doing at this time, except 'Haa! Haa! Haa!' which he could only express in great confusion.

'The Ọba! The Ọba! Huu, huu, huu!' Slanderer continued to pretend.

'The Ọba! The Ọba! The Ọba! But what the Ọba has done to you?'

'The Ọba has given the order! The Ọba has given the order, that all farmers should cut their maize down but one who failed to do so would be killed immediately! Huu! Huu! Huu!' thus Slanderer with his cunnings deceived Pauper and he frightened him as well.

'But what? The Ọba had ordered the farmers to cut their maize down or what are you telling me?' Pauper was shocked in his distorted face.

'It is just so! It is so the Ọba said!' Slanderer stammered.

'But why should the farmers destroy their maize?' Pauper asked in a trembling voice.

'The Ọba said that the locusts were near and that when they came, if they did not see the ears of maize to eat, they would fly away immediately!' Slanderer explained to Pauper in a clear voice as if he had lost all his senses but now he had regained them.

'But, Slanderer, could you agree to cut your maize down while it is not yet ripe? Tell me, Slanderer!' Pauper asked in earnest.

'Haaa! The Ọba's order is a sword! Haa, the Ọba who rules the town! For this reason, I had cut all my own maize down immediately the Ọba had made the order!' Slanderer shouted in shock and in earnest as if he was telling the truth to Pauper.

'You have cut your maize down or what?' Pauper was startled.

'Really, I have cut it all down, because the Ọba emphasized sorrowfully in his order that he would kill the farmer who did not comply with his order!' Slanderer added to Pauper's fear again.

'Haaa! This Ọba's order is bad indeed! Alas, this means all the hard work which I had done on my farm comes to vanity in the end!' Pauper lamented sorrowfully.

'Hun-un. It is just so. Alas, I am fed up as well. But the Ọba's order is a great disaster to every farmer! But to save your life from killing, let us go to your farm now and I will join hands with you to cut all your maize down!' Slanderer added to Pauper's fright.

'Well, let us go and cut all down! But it is a great blow to me to cut down the maize which I planted with my hands and which will be ripe enough in about seven days' time! Haa! Alas!'

'Hun-un! Alas, it is very bad! But I join you in lamenting because, "One should not lament alone! Another man should share it with him!" But Pauper, follow my advice. You should comply with the Ọba's order without a bit of grief, because the order of the Ọba of the town is a two-edged sword!' Thus Slanderer deceived Pauper.

But then in great grief and depression, Pauper stood up. He took his cutlass and he told Slanderer to let them go to his farm and cut his maize down. He did so because he did not understand yet that Slanderer was just jealous of his well-thrived maize, in respect of his own which he planted on the barren land and which was not good.

It took them up to four hours to cut down the whole of the unripe maize. Before Pauper cut two maize down, Slanderer had cut about thirty down. He was perspiring profusely as he was jumping here and there on the farm.

Now, Slanderer became extremely happy to the bottom of his heart when he saw that his wicked cunnings worked successfully. After all Pauper's maize was cut down, they returned to his farmhouse. When they sat down Pauper supported his chin with his left hand and he was thinking sorrowfully about his maize. Slanderer began to pretend to be sympathizing with him. But a little after, he returned to his house in the vicinity of Araromi town.

Now, Slanderer's cunnings had worked more than Pauper's strength, although he was lazy. 'Haa, I am happy now that I, Slanderer, who was a sluggard and Pauper, who is a strong man, are the same now. I have no maize and Pauper has none!' Slanderer derided Pauper when he returned to his house. 'Pauper will admit now that what is called destiny exists!' He continued, 'And as from today, he will believe that it was the destiny of poverty and wretchedness that he chose from Creator when he was coming to earth!' It was like that Slanderer helped Pauper to destroy his maize.

But of course Pauper's poverty and wretchedness were so powerful that they used to infect his crops on the farm so much that they were not yielding well. The maize which he planted in this Araromi town yielded well. But in the long run, Slanderer caused him to lose all as well as he had lost the previous ones. So there was no difference between his former and latter crops.

Now, Pauper was in a great grief. Depression overwhelmed him so much that he was unable to go to his farm any longer.

But one day, when Pauper had expected Slanderer for some days to come and pay a visit to him, according to how they had been doing before, but he did not see him. He thought perhaps he was ill. But as Pauper loved Slanderer as a true friend, he went to his house.

But to Pauper's surprise, he did not meet Slanderer at home. He walked round his house but the only sign that he saw proved that Slanderer had left his house for a long time.

But then he walked further in that area. But he was amazed greatly when he began to see maize on the left and right of the road on which he was travelling. The maize was not cut down at all. When Pauper was very sure that the maize was not cut down, he understood at once that Slanderer had simply deceived him to cut his own maize down but that the Ọba did not give such order to farmers to cut their maize down.

Now, Pauper blamed himself that he should have found out from the other farmers before he allowed Slanderer and himself to cut his maize down.

'Haa, alas! But it is sure that Slanderer and I will meet face to face again! Although it may be sooner or later!' thus Pauper lamented in earnest. However, he returned to his farmhouse, because he knew that, 'hissing precedes weeping; remorse follows a mistake; all the wise men of the country assemble but find no sacrifice for mistake'.

All Pauper's maize had been already cut down and there was nothing that he could do to restore it.

# 18

# PAUPER AND SLANDERER RETURN TO
# OFADAFA'JURO TOWN

But it was not so long before Pauper, with empty hands, returned to Ofadafa'juro town, the town in which he, Brawler and Slanderer lived before the Oba and his chiefs expelled them, when Slanderer called himself a money-doubler and took money from the women.

Pauper and Slanderer had left this town at midnight for another town while they left Brawler there in respect of her brawls. But as Slanderer was a traitor, he did not tell Pauper before he left Araromi town for Ofadafa'juro. Of course, as 'an evil-doer does things with suspicion', so Slanderer knew that what he did to Pauper was extremely bad. So he feared to tell him when he wanted to leave Araromi town.

But when Slanderer returned to Ofadafa'juro town, he asked for clemency from the Oba and his chiefs. Then they pardoned him and they allowed him to live in their town. And when Pauper returned to this town, the Oba and his chiefs pardoned him too to live in the town.

But Pauper wondered indeed when he met Slanderer in this town, without telling him before he left Araromi town.

Although Slanderer was the cause of the destruction of Pauper's maize in Araromi town, he continued to make friends with him in this Ofadafa'juro town. Even their friendship was stronger this time than ever, and they lived in the same house comfortably.

But Pauper 'hid the blood in his stomach and he was spitting the white out'. He hid in his heart the pang of his maize which Slanderer forced him to destroy. But he waited till the day came when he would get the chance to take revenge on him for his maize.

But we should remember that Brawler, Pauper's wife, was still seeking about for her husband. She was not aware till now that her husband and Slanderer had returned to Ọfadafa'juro town in which they left her in the dead-night when they went to Abanirẹ town and then from there to Ararọmi town where they farmed.

In this Ọfadafa'juro town, Pauper returned to his usual wood-carving. But Slanderer, the father of sluggards, with his cunnings, he got the chance to see the Ọba and his chiefs.

Fortunately, he was employed as one of the Ọba's Ikọ or messengers and he was also a tale-bearer for the Ọba and his chiefs. For this, they gave him very poor remuneration and in addition, their useless dresses, as a reward for his busy-body tale-bearing.

It was so Pauper and Slanderer were carrying on their manner of living in this town. But Brawler was still looking about for her husband from one town to another.

# 19

## PAUPER TAKES REVENGE ON SLANDERER ON
## THE DAY OF HIS MARRIAGE

A little time after Slanderer was getting a little money from the Ọba and his chiefs as a remuneration, and useless dresses, he started to court a lady.

The town of this lady was not so far from Ọfadafa'juro town. And it was not so long after he started to court the lady that he began to boast to all the people of the town that there was not a woman in the town who had such beauty as his intended lady.

As Slanderer continued to boast all about, thus he was preparing forcibly for his wedding day as hastily as he could. On Ọjọ-Aṣẹṣẹdaye or Ọjọbọ (The Day of New Creation) in the month of Erele (February), Slanderer paid the dowry of his lady to her parents and they betrothed her to him that very day. And they fixed the marriage day for seven days' time in the same month of Erele.

Before the day was reached, Slanderer had announced to his countless friends that they would accompany him to his lover's town on that day. For as soon as he had become the Ikọ for the Ọba and the chiefs, he was so famous now in the town that he got so many friends at once. But Pauper refused to accompany him as his best man to the town of his in-laws.

Pauper deceived him that he had been warned not to ford streams or rivers in that very month of Erele. But he refused to accompany him just for a certain reason.

The reason was that as Slanderer was preparing to marry his lover, it was so Pauper too was preparing to take revenge on him on the very day of his marriage, in respect of his maize which was destroyed when he (Slanderer) deceived him. Just as 'bat drops its head downwards, keeping watching the way the birds behave', it was so for Pauper. He just kept silent and he was looking at Slanderer how he was preparing forcibly to marry his lover.

Before the day of Slanderer's marriage was reached, Pauper had carved a strange image from light wood. It was a hideous and tawdry image whose appearance was just like an evil spirit. He carved this tawdry image in the size which, when he entered it, would contain him with ease. Its breast could be opened to left and right like two-way sliding doors and it could close jointly when he was inside it.

With the two feet of this hideous image, Pauper could walk here and there and as fast as he wanted to. Its two arms could move up and down or as one who was inside it wished to move both. Its neck could move to left, right, back and front. Pauper carved two fearful eyes on its head with which he could see clearly when he was inside it. He carved two thick horns on its head. Each was coiled like that of a buffalo. Having done all that, he adhered a large quantity of long hair on to its chin and upper lip.

Having done these terrible things on this tawdry image, he painted it from feet to head with various kinds of paints. Now, the image became hideous and a terror of terrors for both children and adults who might see it. Even if a person was as brave as a chisel which cuts its fellow iron, he would be shocked nearly to death immediately he saw this hideous tawdry image.

After Pauper had finished the final touches to this image, he hid it in the forest. But then he made one club of iron and having sharpened his very cutlass with which he cut down his maize when Slanderer deceived him that the Ọba of Aràrọmi town ordered all farmers in his land to cut their maize down, then he kept both club of iron and that cutlass in his room. That was how Pauper prepared himself for the day of Slanderer's marriage.

Well, of course, 'the hawk in the sky does not know that the people below are seeing him'. It was just so for Slanderer. He was going up and down in the town like the waistband or like the beads which are on the waist. He was preparing joyfully for the day of his marriage. But Pauper was silent, he was looking at him and he pretended to be unaware of Slanderer's preparations.

Now, there remained one morning to reach the day of Slanderer's marriage. But when it was the dead-night and when the hands and feet of everybody were at rest, Pauper carried the hideous tawdry image to the road which went to the town of Slanderer's in-laws. He hid it behind one big tree, near that road. After, he hastily returned to the house before daybreak.

When it was daybreak, he began to keep watch when Slanderer, his singers, minstrels, drummers and his friends would leave for his lover's town.

In the morning, the singers, minstrels and drummers gathered in front of the house. After Slanderer and his friends had dressed in beautiful dresses, Pauper stood now on the doorway, he was looking at them. But when it was time to leave, the drummers started to beat their drums, the singers were singing and the minstrels were flattering Slanderer 'in nines and tens'.

Then Slanderer and his friends walked from the house to outside. He and his friends began to dance merrily along to the town of his in-laws. It was like that Slanderer, his friends, drummers, singers and minstrels, otherwise called as from now Slanderer's well-wishers, continued to dance from the town to the town of his in-laws.

When it was about two hours since Slanderer and his well-wishers had left and as the housewives started to cook food for the marriage ceremony, Pauper entered his room. He took his club of iron and his cutlass. He wrapped them up in one rag, he held it and then he left the town, but he went to the big tree behind which he hid the hideous tawdry image. He hid himself under that tree and then he was waiting for the return of Slanderer and his well-wishers, his new wife and her calabash-carriers (bridesmaids) who carried her property.

But as 'there is no bypath on top of the palm tree', Pauper knew well that there was no other road but only this same road on which Slanderer, his well-wishers, his new wife and her family, the calabash-carriers who carried her property, would trek down to Ọfadafa'juro town.

As soon as Slanderer and his friends danced merrily in the house of his in-laws, they began to eat the delicious food of different kinds and they began to drink the palm wine as they wished, without knowing that ill luck was waiting on the road for Slanderer, the bridegroom.

When it was about four o'clock in the evening and from a long distance, Pauper heard the sounds of the drums and the rude song of the drunkards. Now, Pauper knew that Slanderer, his bride and her calabash-carriers and the rest were coming.

When he was sure that they were near, he entered his tawdry image of an evil spirit. Having closed its breast up, he held his cutlass with the left hand while he held his club of iron with the right hand. Now, this image became a vivid evil spirit.

After, he walked to the roadside, he stopped and hid himself there. But soon Slanderer, his bride, the bridesmaids or calabash-carriers with the property of the bride on their heads, friends, singers, drummers and minstrels danced madly to that spot on which the image hid.

Then the image walked wildly on to the road and blocked the road suddenly. Now, they could not go forward or backward. But when this hideous image walked on to the road suddenly and they saw a long cutlass in its left hand and one club of iron on its right hand, they were so afraid that all of them halted on one spot. They were unable to run forward or backward.

'The heavy rain which keeps the birds of the bush in silence', it was just so this terrible image was for Slanderer and the rest. The whole of them so much feared it that the drummers were not aware when they stopped beating their drums. The singers and minstrels also closed their mouths immediately. Slanderer and his friends were so much overwhelmed by the terrible and hostile behaviour of this image that they began to breathe with difficulty immediately and did not know how much more to speak out.

Slanderer's bride and her calabash-carriers were forced to open their mouths but the fear of this image did not let them remember to close them back. But every one of them was just shivering in fear when the image appeared to all of them suddenly.

Immediately Pauper (Image) changed his voice to that of the

evil spirit or monster. He raised his club of iron high up, he shouted terribly in the voice of a hostile monster and then he walked wildly to Slanderer. He said: 'Ho-oo! You, Slanderer! I command you to cut your head away from your neck now! I say now! Now! Because I am extremely thirsty and I want to cool down my thirst with the blood of your head! Now, take this my cutlass!' the Image stretched his cutlass to Slanderer.

'Haa!' with sulky eyes, in fear and trembling, Slanderer stammered, 'This your command is not possible for me at all! I cannot kill myself!' Slanderer shivered in fear, because he had never seen or come across such as this fearful Image since when he was born on earth.

But when he refused to take the cutlass from the Image, then the Image, with all his power, hit his forehead suddenly with his club of iron. After that, he walked wildly up and down on the road. When he walked wildly back to him and the rest of the people, those who feared so much that they were able to move neither their hands nor feet.

The hideous Image stretched his cutlass to Slanderer again. He shouted greatly to him in a horrible voice, he said: 'I say, take this my cutlass and cut your head away from your neck with it! I say, I want to drink the blood! Take my cutlass!'

'Nevertheless I shall cut my head off!' Slanderer shouted in earnest.

'Oh-ho-o! Is that so?' the Image grinned like a madman. 'But you ought to know that "one who admits his guilt in time does not keep long in kneeling down".' The Image shouted horribly to Slanderer. After, with all his power, he struck at his shoulder with his club of iron.

But when Slanderer felt severe pain on his shoulder, willing or not, he took the cutlass from the Image at once. He raised it up to cut off his head but he lowered his hand down when he looked at his bride's face. Instead, to cut his head, he turned his face to the Image. He shook it sorrowfully and then he shouted greatly in pain, he said: 'I say, I cannot cut my head away from my neck!'

Having heard this objection from Slanderer, the Image shouted at him in a shrill voice. Then he walked wildly forward and

94

backward. When he returned to Slanderer, he beat both his shoulders heavily again. After, he told him, 'O-hoo, do you think I am joking with you? Please, cut your head off now, my friend! Make haste! And I close my eyes! But before I open them let me hear the thud of your head on the ground!' The Image grinned in a voice which was terrifying indeed. After, he barked at him like a bull-dog.

'Haa! Hee! Hoo! Please, have mercy on me!' Slanderer despaired. 'The bones of my shoulders have broken!' Slanderer lamented bitterly.

'Hun-un, "the bad people are more numerous than the trees in the bush, but good people are rarer than the eyes". But Slanderer, you are one of the most wicked people who are on earth!' the hideous tawdry Image shouted to Slanderer. Then he clubbed at him again heavily. 'I say, whether you like it or not, you must cut your head away from your neck! Be quick! Otherwise I shall break your head into pieces now! Do you agree to do so or not?' the Image frowned at Slanderer again. After, he barked at him like a dog: 'Waa! Wo-o-o! Woo!'

'Haa, please, I appeal to you! It is not easy at all for one to cut off his own head! Please, I beg you!' Slanderer began to rub his hands at the Image as he was weeping bitterly.

'All right, it isn't too bad yet! But I command you now to behead your bride "in a wink of monkey"! Do the deed now! And let me hear the thud of her head on the ground now! I close my eyes but before I open them you ought to have cut it off her neck! But after you have cut it then you should cut off your own as well! Be ready! I close my eyes now!' The Image grinned and barked at Slanderer in a shrill voice.

'Haa, to behead my bride who belongs to another kin?' Slanderer was greatly startled. But when his bride, the bridesmaids and the rest heard the Image's command this time, they were so much afraid that every one of them hastily grasped his or her head with both hands as if the head had been already cut off.

'I say I cannot cut off my bride's head!' Slanderer lamented.

'What, you Slanderer opened your mouth but you told me that you could not behead your bride or what did you say? He! I don't think you know who you are talking to! Don't you know that you are talking to the living creature of the grass-field who is the terror of terrors and who kills and eats the human being? Ha-ah! But as you have belittled me, take more beats of my club of iron just to warm you up!' The Image then ran at Slanderer suddenly. He clubbed him seven times consecutively.

But the beats were so severe that they made him unconscious and he was not aware when he raised the cutlass up. But as he was lowering his hand just to cut off the head of his bride, the Image hastily pushed the cutlass away from her neck with his club of iron.

After, he remarked to Slanderer loudly that: 'It is improper to behead an unsinning person! It was not your bride who had offended me but it was you!'

Having remarked to Slanderer like that, he struck him again with his club of iron three times consecutively.

Meanwhile, these punishments were overmuch severe for Slanderer, while the behaviours of the Image were becoming more and more hostile. Slanderer's well-wishers, his bride and her calabash-carriers who carried her property, so much feared the Image that they were unable to open their mouths and plead for him perhaps the Image might pardon and release him.

As soon as this hideous tawdry Image took the cutlass back from Slanderer he grinned and made a steady shriek in a strange voice which was very hurtful to the ears of those living creatures who were near that area so that they kept quiet immediately.

'But Slanderer, you should admit that you are just like a tormentor who forces his victim to be cruel!' Having shouted at Slanderer the Image beat at his nape with his usual club of iron.

The Image was just trying to make Slanderer understand about his (Pauper's) maize which he and Slanderer cut down when both of them went and farmed at Araromi town years ago.

'Haa! Ye, ye, ye! But your club pains me so much that my neck is sinking into my shoulders without carrying a load! But with great respect, I beg you, this Spirit (tawdry Image of the evil spirit), even if I had offended you before! Please, forgive me!' Slanderer pleaded in great agony.

But then when Slanderer could no longer bear these severe sufferings and as tears were rolling down his cheeks, he looked at the faces of his friends, minstrels, drummers and singers and of his bride and her calabash-carriers and then he hastily winked at them, perhaps they could help him to overpower the Image. But instead of helping him, they dropped their heads down and then they fastened their eyes on the ground in great fear.

But the monstrous Image did not accept his plea. Instead, as he was jumping fiercely here and there like a hungry tiger, so he was rushing furiously against Slanderer, and threatening him and so he was beating him continuously with his club of iron.

'Slanderer, I want you to understand that, "old age has no remedy"! Hereby, there is no way for you to escape my revenge!' After, he rushed furiously against him. He pretended to butt him in his stomach to death with the thick coiled horns on his head.

Indeed, even if Slanderer was a clever, cunning, treacherous and perfidious person who had no rivals on earth, all this could not save him from these severe punishments at all.

'But if you club me for two minutes more, I shall die!' Slanderer despaired bitterly when the Image clubbed him again.

'You lie! You cannot die because the Ọba of Laketu town has changed you from mortal to immortal in the name of Creator before he expelled you!' the Image reminded Slanderer in a fearful voice and then he rushed furiously against him.

'And "what makes a dog bark is not sufficient to make a sheep gaze". Do you hear me, Slanderer? These punishments which I am giving you today are not up to ten per cent of what you had done to me years ago, which I hid in my mind without telling it out to anybody!' the Image roared angrily.

'Please, I beg you in the name of the king of spirits! Whatever I had done to you, forgive me!' Slanderer pleaded in confusion and in tears.

'Nevertheless I shall forgive you!' the Image shouted. 'Haa! You, Slanderer's bride, I want you to be sure that your husband will cut his head away from his neck today! It is not you who had offended me, so it is not proper to punish innocent person! For this reason, I command you and your calabash-carriers who are carrying your property to go back to your town now! But you should put it in your mind that Slanderer is no more your husband as from today! All right, let you all go away now! Goodbye!' It was like that Slanderer's bride and her calabash-carriers or bridesmaids were set free.

But Slanderer's bride and her bridesmaids had hardly heard this command from the hideous tawdry Image when the calabash-carriers hastily threw down the property of the bride and then they and the bride took to their heels. As they were running fiercely back to their town it was so they were thanking Creator for delivering them from the Image which they took to be an evil spirit. But as all were running along desperately for their lives, it was so Slanderer began to look at his bride with half an eye until all had disappeared on the road.

As soon as his bride had disappeared from his sight, he turned his face to the Image, the terror of terrors. Weeping bitterly, he made a vow that: 'But if you can forgive me my offence, I shall atone you with one big fat he-goat! Please, I beg you!'

'Haaa! "He who pelts another with stones invites metal in return." Therefore, I refuse your sacrifice! I don't want your he-goat or any other kind of a sacrifice whatsoever you may offer to me! But the only thing that I want you to do is to cut your head onto the ground now. Otherwise I'll help you cut it off! Take, this is the cutlass!' The Image refused Slanderer's sacrifice but he stretched the cutlass to him instead.

But when Slanderer feared so much that he could not take the cutlass from the Image, the Image struck at his nape again much with his club of iron three times and then he fell upon the ground, sprawling. But when he struggled and stood up wobbling, he begged the Image to help him call his bride back to carry her property away, which her calabash-carriers threw down before they fled away in fear.

'By the way, what is the name of that your ex-bride?'

'Her name is QMQLERE (meaning, child is reward),' Slanderer replied bitterly.

'Is that so? All right! "It is only bent but it isn't yet damaged." I shall help you call your bride back but that will be after you have cut away your head from your neck!' The Image gave him some beats of the club again. Then he made a mockery of him.

'But as you refuse to take the cutlass from me, now, all that I want you to do first before you behead yourself is that I want your drummers to start to beat their drums, your singers to start to sing and then you should begin to dance to the drums to and fro in front of me. But in addition, you should be laughing joyfully for me! It is just like that I want you to amuse me first!'

'What? To dance and laugh joyfully for you?' Slanderer wondered and murmured with sulky eyes. 'But after you have nearly beaten me to death and moreover you have driven Ọmọlere, my beautiful bride, away! Haaa, no! I cannot do so at all!' Slanderer murmured sadly. After, he continued to weep bitterly.

'O-ho-o-o! Slanderer, I warn you! Don't go beyond your boundary! But it will be better for you if you start to do what will amuse me now and that which will make me laugh! Otherwise you will get more beats of the club!' the Image warned Slanderer angrily.

'Haa, Slanderer, but it will be better for you to dance and laugh for this bad spirit (Image) than for him to continue to beat you!' Slanderer's friends, singers, drummers and minstrels or poets, those who had been kept quiet by fear since this disaster had befallen Slanderer became alive now. Then they advised him. But he did not follow their advice.

But when the Image struck him again several times, willing or not, Slanderer started to dance and laugh reluctantly as the drummers were beating their drums and the singers were singing for him:

Jo'jo iya k'awo o – Panla ṣe'gun sai – saisai!
Dance the dance of suffering and let's see it!
Jo'jo iya k'awo o – Panla ṣe'gun sai – saisai!
Dance the dance of suffering and let's see it!
Jo'jo iya k'awo o – Panla ṣe'gun sai – saisai!

But as Slanderer was dancing sluggishly and was laughing like a madman and as his dance was not conforming to the beats of the

99

drums, the Image became wild suddenly and then in great annoyance, he clubbed his shoulders so heavily that he fell down and then he began to lament for pain.

Soon, he stood up with much difficulty. But as he was wobbling painfully, the Image commanded the drummers again to change the beats of their drums to that of Ṣango, the god of thunder, and the singers to change their song to that of Ṣango as well for Slanderer to dance to it.

But then without hesitation and in fear, the drummers and singers started:

At 'Ọmọlere at' Arugba – Mo gba a – Mo gba a tan porogodo
   Mo gba a!
Both Ọmọlere and the Calabash-carriers – I take them – I take
   them altogether – I take them all!
At 'Ọmọlere at' Arugba – Mo gba a – Mo gba a tan porogodo
   Mo gba a!
Both Ọmọlere and the Calabash-carriers – I take them – I take
   them altogether – I take them all!
At 'Ọmọlere at' Arugba – Mo gba a – Mo gba a tan porogodo
   Mo gba a!
Both Ọmọlere and the Calabash-carriers – I take them – I take
   them altogether – I take them all!
At 'Ọmọlere at' Arugba – Mo gba a – Mo gba a tan porogodo
   Mo gba a – Mo gba a tan porogodo
   Mo gba a!

But after Slanderer had danced the dance of suffering sluggishly and laughed like a madman he began to dance the dance of Ṣango to the Image but with reluctance, when the Image struck at his forehead with his club of iron in anger.

Now, having adjusted himself, Slanderer hastily danced this dance of the Ṣango worshipper even far better than the Ṣango worshipper. And too, he kicked the air so accurately that his dance matched the beats of the drums. Because 'the Ṣango worshipper who dances and does not kick the air belittles himself'.

Slanderer had hardly danced the dance of Ṣango when the Image clubbed him three times consecutively. But now he felt such pain that he shouted greatly at the topmost of his voice and he appealed to whoever might be near there: 'Please, all beings of the bush and beings of the road! Come and save me from this evil spirit (Image)! He is beating me nearly to death! Please, come to my aid now!'

But immediately Slanderer despaired and lamented in great pain like that, Pauper opened the breast of his tawdry image to left and right like two-way sliding doors. He came out from it with a broad smile. But then he began to look at Slanderer steadfastly.

'Haa-ha! Is it you?' Slanderer, his friends, drummers, singers and minstrels took a full breath as their eyes were dazed.

'O, yes, it is I!' Pauper shrugged and replied simply with a smile.

'But what you have done to me today was too bad!' Slanderer shook his head to left and right. Then in great sorrow, he accused Pauper.

'But you too had done the worst to me in the days gone by!' Pauper made a mockery of Slanderer in a smile.

'But what sort of a bad thing had I done to you in the days gone by which forced you to punish me so severely? After, you let me lose Ọmọlere, my beautiful bride!' Having asked sorrowfully like that, Slanderer began to weep bitterly for his sad fate.

'Thank you! It is so we ought to ask. ''One who has evacuated his bowels has forgotten, but one who has cleared it away has not forgotten it!'' But you Slanderer, could you remember now that once upon a time, because your maize did not thrive well like my own, you were so jealous of mine and with your wicked cunnings you deceived me that the Ọba of Araromi town gave an order that all farmers in his land should cut their maize down?'

Pauper continued to remind Slanderer of his cruel behaviours, he said: 'You told me that day that you and I should go to my farm and help me cut my maize down, so that the Ọba might not kill me! But then both of us destroyed my maize that day!' Thus Pauper reminded Slanderer of his evil deed when both of them went to farm at Araromi town.

'Ho-o-o, yes, yes! I remember now that it was so I deceived you that day!' Slanderer confessed sluggishly.

'But as it was a great grief to me,' Pauper went further in his allegation, 'about that my maize, the right action which I would have taken was to kill you rightout today. But it is not good to pay bad for bad!' Pauper frowned.

But as soon as Pauper had reminded Slanderer like that he turned his back to Slanderer suddenly and he faced the town. He began to run furiously along to the town as he was saying loudly: '"He who pelts another with stones invites metal in return." '

It was like that Slanderer's evil cunnings caused him to lose his beautiful Ọmọlere and moreover he was badly punished nearly to death for his cruel characters.

Just a little after that Slanderer, his friends, drummers, singers and minstrels left the town in the morning for his bride's town, the housewives had started to cook plenty of food for Slanderer's marriage feast. And several kegs of the palm wine were also provided.

As time was getting nearer, it was so the people of Ọfadafa'juro town were gathering more and more in front of the house in which Slanderer and Pauper lived. They were expecting Slanderer and his friends to arrive with the bride. Also, the Ọba and his chiefs had prepared themselves ready in their palaces to do their own part in Slanderer's marriage ceremony, because he was one of the important tale-bearers and Ikọ for the Ọba and his chiefs.

'The bat hangs down its head and is watching the behaviour of the birds.' It was just so for Pauper who lived in the same house with Slanderer. He kept silent and then he was watching the crowd of people who were rushing to the front of the house. All were waiting anxiously to see how beautiful Slanderer's bride was, because he had been boasting to the people for the last six months that he was courting a lady and that there was none of the women in the town who was as beautiful as she was.

After Pauper had left for the town, Slanderer, his friends, drummers, minstrels and singers, all of them gathered together on the very spot on which Pauper had punished Slanderer.

But as Pauper had driven Slanderer's bride away, for this reason, he could not bring her to the town. But he, his friends, drummers, singers and minstrels were much overwhelmed with

102

shame and they were greatly confused by what to do. They did not know what to tell the people why they did not bring the bride.

They were still in this confusion for a while when one of Slanderer's friends said: 'By the way, what are we going to tell the people of the town has caused our failure to bring the bride with us to the town?'

But then one of the drummers said with his drum: 'That will be a great shame for us if the people don't see the bride with us!' Again, one of the minstrels recited in her poems: '"This is the place where three roads meet and which puzzles a stranger." '

But when all of them thought over and over but they did not know what they could do to suppress the shame for them, Slanderer, with his usual cunnings, cut in suddenly. He told his friends and the others that: 'There is no problem of shame for us at all. But "if we cannot get the forest-bat for the sacrifice, we should use the house-bat for the sacrifice".'

Then without hesitation, Slanderer loosened his bride's boxes which contained women dresses, and which were thrown on the ground before the calabash-carriers and the bride fled. He pulled out one beautiful wrapper, one head-tie, one neck-coral beads, one veil and two bracelets from the boxes.

Then Slanderer put the coral-beads on his neck, he put each of the two bracelets on each of his wrists. He wrapped himself from the breast down to his knees with the wrapper, he wore the woman's short loose garment, he wound the head-tie round his head and then he covered his head to the breast with the veil. Having dressed like that, Slanderer was not different from the bride who was on the way to her bridegroom's house. It was like that Slanderer disguised himself as his bride.

After, he told his friends to line up at his back, then the drummers, singers and minstrels to start their amusements and follow them while he was in front of all like a bride.

But when all of them danced to the town, the crowd of people shouted greatly in joy. They began to rush here and there, shouting: 'The bride has come! The bride has come!' Everyone was trying to see Slanderer's new wife, whom he had been boasting of to the people that she was more beautiful than any of the women in the town.

Well, as 'a town is never so small without having a dunghill', is so according to the marriage tradition of Ọfadafa'juro town, as soon as Slanderer was accompanied to the doorway like a bride, the housewives hastily filled to the brim one large bowl with water. They brought it to the doorway. But when the housewives began to wash his feet in the bowl, they observed immediately that the feet were that of a man and not of a woman.

But as soon as the drummers, minstrels, singers and Slanderer's friends were sure that there was no way, Slanderer's cunning would soon be outwitted, all of them did as 'the pond, which stands aloof from the stream as if it does not relate to it' did. So they began to bolt away one after the other as they were winking to one another. And within one minute the whole of them had bolted away. But now, there remained Slanderer alone, who disguised himself as his bride.

But when the crowd of people did not hear the beats of the drums, singing and the reciting of the poems suddenly, which were the most important for Slanderer's wedding, they were confused by what had happened.

But after the housewives had washed Slanderer's feet with suspicion, they stood upright. And according to the tradition, they wanted to remove the veil away from his face for the people to see the face of the bride. But to keep the secret within himself, Slanderer did not allow the housewives to remove the veil. Instead, he held it onto his face with both hands.

But Pauper who stood near the doorway and was keeping watch on the activities of the housewives all the while, was not aware when he burst into great laughter. When the wrestling between Slanderer and the housewives continued, then this time the crowd of the spectators rushed to them and they gathered round them just to see what was happening.

Being 'an elder who goes to excess loses respect', is that as the housewives continued to wrestle with Slanderer in order to remove his veil for the people to see his face, and they could not overpower him, Pauper ran to the doorway. 'In a wink of crab', he tore the veil into pieces and then he pulled it away from Slanderer's face.

Now, 'the tiger is at large; it is seen by everybody, there can be no secret about it any more'. The crowd of people saw now that it was Slanderer who had disguised himself as his bride.

But when the people shouted greedily on Slanderer, he was so ashamed that he covered his face with both his hands. Then he hastily escaped into the bush that night. But at the same time, everything turned into confusion. The people did not understand why Slanderer disguised himself as his bride.

However, as soon as shame had driven Slanderer into the bush, the people ate all the food and drank the palm wine which had been prepared for the ceremony of his wedding. After, everyone went back to his or her house disappointed, as the whole of them were making mockery of him.

It was like that Slanderer lost his bride, Ọmọlere, in the end in respect of his wicked cunnings.

Slanderer returned to the town after ten days that he had escaped with shame into the bush. But inasmuch as he was a habitual treacherous man of that century, he brought with him Brawler, Pauper's brawling wife, to the town. Not knowing that when he escaped into the bush that night, but later, he started to go from one town to another, searching for Brawler.

But what had caused him to bring Brawler back to Ọfadafa'juro town at all costs was that he wanted to take revenge on Pauper in respect of the severe punishments which he had suffered from Pauper on the day of his wedding. Because he knew well that his bringing Brawler back would be a great problem to her husband.

But, 'How many can we count from Adepele's muddled teeth? He has one hundred side teeth, forty front teeth, and four hundred and forty molars hidden at the back of his mouth.' It was so for Slanderer. His unforeseen evil characters were uncountable. And that was how Slanderer used Brawler as an instrument to punish her husband.

# 20

# PAUPER, BRAWLER AND SLANDERER FLEE
# FROM ỌFADAFA'JURO TOWN

Now, Slanderer had returned to the town and he resumed his usual duties as the Ọba's Ikọ or messenger and tale-bearer. But he was putting Pauper in troubles continuously for he punished him and then he caused him to lose his bride on the day of his wedding, and also he was putting the people of the town in troubles every day.

Even, as time went on, Slanderer was so well established in a favourable position in Ọfadafa'juro town, so he began to cause confusions for the Ọba and his chiefs. He turned everything into great chaos in the town of Ọfadafa'juro, the town which was in great settlement for centuries.

But as 'it is risky to tell the secret to a treacherous person', so Slanderer, knowing all the secrets of the Ọba and his chiefs, began to use this opportunity to cause much misunderstandings on them. And within a few months he caused them to be the enemies of one another.

Slanderer was also telling lies to the chiefs that the Ọba was enticing their wives with money and by that he used to have sex with them. Having heard this serious allegation from Slanderer, all the chiefs boycotted the Ọba and the Aafin, or palace.

As Slanderer was using his wicked cunnings to cause serious confusions in the town it was so Brawler was causing confusions in the house and the neighbourhood every day with her harmful brawls. And so Slanderer was receiving the bribes from the guilty and the guiltless people.

But at last, when the Ọba scrutinized the sudden confusions which were nearly ruining his town at this time, he knew that it was Slanderer who was causing the incident to him, his chiefs and to the people of the town as a whole. But just as 'when the elders are in the market, a child's head will not be allowed to bend to the wrong side', for this reason, the Ọba summoned all his chiefs to an emergency meeting in his Aafin. He told them that it was Slanderer who was the man who was causing the confusions and the misunderstandings.

But after they had settled their misunderstandings amicably, then they resolved that the punishment which Slanderer deserved for his misdeed, was to sacrifice him along with Pauper and Brawler to the Ọba's Ogun or god of iron, in the morning of the coming Ọjọ-Ẹti (The Day of Trouble – Friday).

Although Pauper and Brawler, his wife, had committed no offence, both were sojourners like Slanderer, and that was the reason they were to be atoned to the Ogun along with Slanderer. But of course, 'what affects the eyes will affect the nose'.

After the Ọba with his chiefs had planned their deed in secrecy like that, the chiefs returned to their houses and they did not tell anybody this their deed.

But before the Ọjọ-Ẹti had arrived, one of Pauper's friends, who overheard this secret deed, advised him, Brawler and Slanderer to flee from Ọfadafa'juro town before that day of Ọjọ-Ẹti, otherwise they would lose their lives.

When Pauper's friend had hinted him so, he told Brawler and Slanderer what the Ọba and his chiefs were preparing to do for them on the coming Ọjọ-Ẹti (The Day of Trouble – Friday). But when Slanderer heard this from Pauper, he told him immediately that they should flee from the town in the night of Ọjọ-Iṣẹgun (The Day of Victory – Tuesday).

But being 'ajao' has not any property to pack when it is leaving a place', it is just so for Pauper. His destiny of poverty and wretchedness did not let him have any other property more than the dirty rags which were on his body. And so for Brawler, her own predestination was hurtful brawls. Brawls did not let her have any other property as well besides her brawls.

When the day they wanted to flee arrived, 'in a wink of crab'

Pauper and Brawler put their rags, cutlass, axe and their soup-pot in a worn-out basket which they were using as their box.

Although sloth was among Slanderer's uncountable evil characters which he had chosen from Creator when he was coming to earth, he was the Ọba's and the chiefs' Ikọ and tale-bearer. This helped him to have useless trousers, garments and caps which the Ọba and the chiefs were giving him as a reward.

So, without hesitation, he put all those useless clothes on his large cover-cloth. He rolled it up into a bundle. Then he put the bundle on his head and so Brawler too put their worn-out basket on her head. Then the three of them fled from Ọfadafa'juro town in that dead-night.

Just a few hours after they had left that town behind, they went direct to one town which was on the east.

# 21

# PAUPER, BRAWLER AND SLANDERER
# BECOME SLAVES IN AIKU TOWN

Having travelled for about seven days, Pauper, Brawler and Slanderer came to one town called AIKU and it was on the east of that area. But then the three of them started to live in this town.

The most important work which the men were doing there was to go to the neighbouring towns to capture people. When they brought them to their town, Aiku, then they would sell them into slavery.

But as there were no big trees which Pauper could use for carving into various kinds of things, because this Aiku town was on grass-field, this forced him to join the men who were capturing other people as slaves. So, one morning, he followed the men who were going to capture people from one town. But all of them had not travelled far when Slanderer and Brawler began to run after them. When they overtook them, Pauper and the other men asked from Brawler and Slanderer: 'But where are you going to?'

'We are following you to capture people as well!' Brawler and Slanderer replied.

'But you should not put us in trouble!' the men and Pauper warned them seriously.

'Haa! Not at all! But we shall not put you in trouble!' Brawler and Slanderer promised.

But then, after the whole of them had travelled for three hours, as Brawler was brawling along the road continuously, they saw a large number of people, women and men, who were running helter-skelter towards them.

'But why are all of you running fiercely like this?' the men and Pauper asked those people.

'Haa, the slave raiders are chasing us to catch! Better you all go back in time so that they might not capture you as slaves!' the people warned them.

But 'in a wink of crab' the slave raiders were seen far off in the opposite direction. But now everything turned into a great confusion suddenly. The matter had become now, 'If you cannot run, leave the way for me'. So they scattered into the different hiding-places in the nearby bush. Everyone lay down flatly without talking or making noise.

But as the whole of them lay down flatly, but at this very delicate time, Brawler started her brawls loudly and suddenly. The rest of the people were waving hands in fear to her to stop or to keep quiet. But Brawler would not stop her brawls until the raiders travelled to the very place in which they hid.

As soon as the raiders heard Brawler's brawls, they knew that some people were hiding themselves in that bush. But then without hesitation, all of them rushed into that bush and they started to search for them. A few minutes later, they found Brawler and they held her at once. But when they wanted to go away with her, she told them that her husband and many other people were still hiding there.

Having searched and searched the bush they found out her husband and Slanderer. But they failed to find out the rest of the people. It was so the slave raiders took Brawler, Slanderer and Pauper away that day.

Now, this proves that indeed 'there is no remedy for unfortunate destiny', as Pauper was already destined for poverty and wretchedness he was captured as a slave instead of capturing people as he intended to do. But in the end, the slave raiders sold the three of them into slavery to one slave-buyer.

But while Slanderer and Pauper were working hard for their buyer, Brawler's hurtful brawls did not let her work at all. But when their master was entirely fed up with her brawls, he sold her cheaply in anger to another slave-buyer who was in another town.

And it was not so long when Brawler had been resold, that Slanderer, with the help of his cunnings, escaped. But then there remained only Pauper who was serving their master now. But having served his master for a few months and his master having appreciated his hard work, he allowed him to pay a small amount of money for his ransom or redemption. Then with happiness Pauper paid the small amount of money which he had saved to his master and then he was set free.

That was how everything which Pauper did brought a deadlock to him in the end. But he never believed that destiny existed at all.

So, he returned to the same Aiku town in which he, his wife and Slanderer were living before all of them were captured and sold into slavery. But he was very surprised when he met Slanderer in the same house in which they were living before the three of them were captured and sold into slavery.

However, he and Slanderer continued to live together in that house as before. But he never knew whereabouts Brawler, his wife, was.

But as 'hunger does not bother whether there is any money in hand; but one feels hunger every day', so when Pauper returned to Aiku town, he began to feel hunger nearly to death. Because he got no any work to do in this barren town, although he was strong indeed.

One day, when Pauper sat down, in anguish of mind, he said: 'In fact, I do not admit that it was the destiny of poverty and wretchedness that I chose from Creator. But since I am unfortunate in everything that I am doing, I shall put more efforts into working harder than before!' It was thus Pauper, with doubtful mind, encouraged himself.

# 22

# PAUPER BECOMES A TRADER IN OWODE TOWN

Very soon, Pauper left Aiku town, he went to another town called OWODE. But later, Slanderer followed him. The two of them were living in the same house. The chief work which the people of Owode town were doing was trading. The land there was very rich for such crops as beans, maize, rice, pepper, etc.

One large river joined this Owode town to the town called Atẹpẹ. Large canoes were used to carry these foodstuffs to Atẹpẹ town. There they sold them for exorbitant prices, because these kinds of foodstuffs were rare for the people of Atẹpẹ town.

Just a few days after Pauper and Slanderer had arrived in Owode town, Brawler saw her husband, Pauper, and then she came to live with him at once. Although she was resold into slavery but at last her brawls were overmuch so that she was entirely useless to do any work. The last slave-buyer who bought her in Owode town drove her away in anger when he could no longer tolerate her hurtful brawls. But then she began to live in this town before Pauper and Slanderer came there.

But now, Pauper, the Father of Wretchedness, wanted to try trading, perhaps it would be favourable to his destiny and perhaps his destiny of poverty and wretchedness would not infect this sort of business, as they had infected all his crops on the farm. But at the same time he was dejected when he remembered that he had no money with which to buy the foodstuffs and no money to pay for hiring the canoe with which to carry the commodities to Atẹpẹ town where he would sell them.

One morning, however, Pauper went to the port and he started to help the traders load their commodities into their canoes. Then in the evening, he told one of the traders to help him get the foodstuffs and the hiring of one canoe on credit. Luckily that trader agreed to help him. But she told him to come back to her the following morning. Pauper was very happy when he was sure that this trader was prepared to help him.

It was hardly the following morning when Pauper went to the woman. Then she took him to the seller of the foodstuffs who sold all to him on credit. Again, this same woman trader took him to a canoe-owner from whom he hired the vessel on credit as well.

But then it took Pauper one full day to load the whole of his commodities into the canoe. After, he employed six paddle-men on credit as well. But when it was nine o'clock in the night, many passengers came to the port and he arranged all of them on top of the commodities, as well as many other traders put their passengers on top of their commodities.

But as Pauper's canoe was just preparing to leave the port along with many other canoes which were more than forty, Brawler and Slanderer came. They told him that they wanted to follow him to Atẹpẹ town. Although he refused them to follow him they forced themselves to enter the canoe. However, he put them on top of the commodities as well.

At ten o'clock prompt, Pauper's canoe left the port along with the other canoes. All the canoes were moving along swiftly on the water because there were no strong tides and breeze at that time. And according to the traditional behaviour of the canoe passengers, they began to sing joyfully as the canoe was moving along smoothly. But Brawler was brawling hotly and continuously instead of singing with those happy passengers.

Before daybreak, Pauper's canoe and the others were nearing Atẹpẹ town. But when it was about three o'clock in the morning, the passengers began to be fed up with Brawler's harmful brawls. And when it was seven o'clock, the passengers could no longer endure her brawls. They were entirely fed up with her brawls.

Meanwhile, brawls were so much intoxicating Brawler that she

113

stood up from her seat. She started to walk up and down in the canoe and it was so she was wilfully trampling the passengers, so, fight and uproar began between her and the passengers unexpectedly. Brawler engaged herself with the passengers and they too engaged themselves with her.

As they were beating Brawler and she too was beating them, Slanderer stood up and he joined Brawler in beating the passengers instead of parting them or settling the misunderstanding for them. But because the fight was tough they were not aware when they rushed to one side of the canoe. Then the canoe bent heavily to that side.

But as there just remained one hundred metres for the canoe to land on the Atẹpẹ port, it broke into two suddenly. Then without hesitation, it sank into the water together with the commodities and all the people in it.

And it was with great difficulty that the other traders who had landed their own canoes safely on the port rescued Pauper, his paddle-men and a few of the passengers onto the port. But the strong tides carried away Brawler, Slanderer, the rest of the passengers and the whole of Pauper's commodities.

'Haaa, I lose in trading as well!' Pauper grasped his head with both hands and then he despaired loudly in earnest when he became conscious. 'Or it is true that it is the destiny of poverty and wretchedness that I chose from Creator as the Babalawo, the Ifa priest, had said when he read my "ẹsẹnt'aye" on the third day that I was born?' Now it seems that Pauper wants to believe that destiny exists. But he is not yet very sure.

'But you, Pauper, did you ask first whether your head has the luck of trading or not before you started it?' the other traders who rescued Pauper asked him.

'Haaa, it is a pity! But I did not ask my head!' Pauper despaired in earnest.

'Well, if you have not asked your head first before you started trading, you have made a great mistake then!' the other traders blamed Pauper, and after they had sympathized with him for his loss they warned him not to attempt trading any longer. But then all of them scattered away.

It was thus all Pauper's efforts to become a trader came to vanity as well in the end.

'Haaa! the best thing for me to do now is to flee somewhere or else if I go back to Owode town, there is no doubt, the owner of the canoe and the seller who sold the foodstuffs to me on credit will tear me into pieces if I fail to pay her money, and so for the owner of the canoe which I hired on credit.'

After Pauper had lamented sorrowfully like that, he stood, he started to stagger along to an unknown destination just like a dead and alive man till he staggered into one wilderness. This wilderness was about forty kilometres from Atẹpẹ town. But till now, he never knew whether the tides which had carried away his wife, Brawler, Slanderer, and many passengers had lost all of them entirely.

# 23

# PAUPER IS INSTALLED THE ỌBA
# OF THE TOWN OF WOMEN

When Pauper, the Father of Wretchedness, had wandered in great grief in this fearful thick wilderness for about six months, without having better food to eat, one day, it came to his mind to make one bow and arrows. And he made all with strong sticks. Then he started to kill the small animals which he ate as he continued to wander about.

One day, he wandered to where there were two mighty mahogany trees in this wilderness. These two trees were at a little distance from each other. But because Pauper was tired and weak this day, he sat at the foot of one of the two trees. After he put his bow and the quiver of his arrows on the left, he leaned his back on the mahogany tree. But as 'sleep does not know death', so as soon as the cool breeze started to blow on him, he was not aware when he was fast asleep.

Pauper enjoyed the sleep so much that it was already noon before he woke suddenly. But as soon as he rubbed his eyes with the back of his right hand and then he looked round that area, to his fear, he saw one feeble old woman who emerged suddenly from the back of the second mahogany tree.

The appearance of this feeble old woman frightened Pauper so much that he hastily took his bow and the quiver. But just as he wanted to run away for his life, the old woman screamed loudly in anger. She said: 'Hee, you this hunter must not run away but you should come to me now at the foot of this tree on which I am standing!'

'Haaa, to come to you?' Pauper asked in a trembling voice.

'I say, you should come to me here otherwise you will find

yourself where you don't expect yourself to be!' The feeble old woman continued her warning, she said: 'And you will continue to wander about in your usual poverty and wretchedness which are your destiny and which embitter your manner of living every day!' The old woman warned Pauper again in peevishness as she supported her weak back with both hands.

'But – but, a human being with the hair on head that I am!' in fear, Pauper described himself and then he moved back a bit. For he took this old woman to be the spirit of that mahogany tree.

'Shut up your mouth there and stop your excuse! But just come to me freely!' she shouted in anger.

'But by the way, for what reason am I fearing death? A man without any purpose that I am! If I can die let me die at once!' Pauper despaired for he had forgotten at this moment that he, Brawler and Slanderer had been immortalized by the Ọba of Laketu town on the day the three of them were expelled from there. But then he shook his head in sorrow and breathed out the breath of grief. After, he walked without fear to the feeble old woman. But when she embraced him, he feared her greatly and he nearly fainted.

'But how did you manage to come into this dreadful thick wilderness?' the old woman asked Pauper in an attractive voice this time as she held him.

'Haaa! Let me tell you the truth. I was driven into this wilderness by poverty and wretchedness!' Pauper explained with throbbing heart.

'Poverty and wretchedness or what?' the old woman wondered.

'Just so. But the people are saying that the destiny which I had chosen from Creator are poverty and wretchedness!' Pauper said sorrowfully.

'Hun – un!' the feeble old woman hummed. 'But where is your town or village?' she released Pauper and asked.

'Haaa! Iya arugbo (old mother), my town is far away from this wilderness just as the sky is far from the ground!'

'Is that so? But what had caused you to leave your town and come to the out-of-doors as this one?' the old woman asked as she bent a bit forward and fastened her eyes on Pauper.

'It was my wife, Brawler, who had caused the Ọba and chiefs of my town to expel me and her out of the town after they had cursed upon us in the name of Creator!'

'The name of your wife is Brawler or what?' wondered the feeble old woman.

'Yes, her name is Brawler!' Pauper confirmed.

'But where is your wife, Brawler, at present?'

'Well, I cannot say exactly where she is now or whether she has gone out of existence together with one my close friend. Because I have not seen any of them from the day that my hired canoe which all of us boarded sank and the tides carried them away!'

'O, pity! I am very sad to hear that your canoe sank and the tides carried your wife and friend away! Sorry!' the feeble old woman sympathized with Pauper for a few minutes.

'But what is your name?' asked the old woman.

'My name is Pauper, the Father of Wretchedness, but sometimes people call me Pauper!'

'Hun – un, wonderful! Well, let me tell you about myself! You see, I am the senior Ọba-maker (king-maker), of the town which was formerly called Town of Glory. But at present it is called the Town of Women!' Iya Arugbo, or feeble old woman who we know now as the senior Ọba-maker, continued her story. She said: 'But if you can follow me to my town, you will forget immediately your poverty and wretchedness which are punishing you about all days!'

But as soon as this senior Ọba-maker explained herself to Pauper in the mode of a human being, then Pauper was very sure now that she was a human being and by that his fear was dispelled. And then, in happiness, he started to follow this senior Ọba-maker from that mahogany tree to her town which was not so far from the wilderness.

When Pauper and the senior Ọba-maker walked abreast into the town, even though this Town of Women was strange to him, he wondered greatly when the multitude of girls, ladies, young women and old women rushed out and met him and the senior Ọba-maker. Some were embracing him warmly while many were scrambling him with the shouts of joy.

'But why are all of you scrambling me? Or are you going to kill me or how?' Pauper was embarrassed.

'Never, but we are not going to kill you!' the multitude of women assured Pauper. 'But we are taking you to the Aafin (palace) of our Ọba!' the women shouted.

But as these women and the senior Ọba-maker were taking Pauper along to the Aafin, he started to notice this Town of Women how it was very beautiful. Of course the senior Ọba-maker had foretold Pauper that the former name of their town was Town of Glory during the time that Peace and Joy came and lived with them there.

But Peace and Joy hastily left there for another peaceful and joyful town when there was rebellion in this Town of Glory. But of course, as 'no matter how poor a prince is, there will still remain in him the sign of the prince', so this reason caused the sign of a bit of peace and joy to remain in this town till that time.

What had caused Peace and Joy to quit this Town of Glory was that Peace and Joy hated to live in a town or house in which there were rebellion, confusion, chaos, brawls, poverty, wretchedness, restlessness of mind, etc.

But we should not forget that Joy was the relative of Brawler's mother while Peace was the relative of Pauper's mother in Laketu town. The two of them had once lived with Pauper and Brawler for many years. But both of them left the couple in sorrow when Pauper's poverty and wretchedness and Brawler's brawls were too much for them to bear.

After a while, Pauper was led into the Aafin and he observed immediately that it was certain there was no Ọba in the Aafin for several years. However they gave him a seat and he was seated with the dirty rags on his body like a madman. His bow and the quiver were yet on his left shoulder.

But before the women in the Aafin, who were the Olori or queens, told their problems to Pauper, they went to the kitchen, they began to prepare the nice food. But soon after the Olori went to the kitchen Pauper looked round the Aafin in which he sat. But he was not aware when wonder forced him to guess:

119

'Am I Pauper? Pauper of yesterday or which? No! Not so! Or am I dreaming? Certainly, it is a dream that I am dreaming!'

Pauper continued his guessing, he said: 'See how the multitude of women are singing and dancing and shouting in great joy for me! But for what reason they are doing all this for me?' Pauper was guessing as if he was not conscious. 'Or these women,' Pauper went on in his guessing, 'are doing all this for me in respect of my poverty and wretchedness?' Then he looked at his right and left again. He did as if he was intoxicated, 'Haa! I don't understand this at all!' It was so Pauper contined to guess when the Olori set the food in the royal dining hall for him.

But when Pauper started at the food, each of his morsels was bigger than his throat. So each time that he gulped each morsel it was so his throat made a very heavy sound. And it was so he was glancing this way and that way savagely as if he were a madman.

Having gulped the food and drunk the hot drink faster than necessary to his satisfaction, then the junior Ọba-makers led him into the bathroom. Having removed all his dirty rags away from his body and also his bow and the quiver, they scraped the hair of his head and that of his chin which was just like that of a madman. Then they washed all his body thoroughly though it wasted a lot of soap but the junior Ọba-makers did not bother about that.

After, they led him into the royal dressing room. But as the tradition of the Town of Women was, the Ọba-makers covered him from head to feet with a very large cover cloth. But now Pauper could not see and he never knew why they were doing all these strange things for him.

# 24

## THE GROVE OF ENTHRONEMENT

According to the primitive custom of the Town of Women, there was a sacred grove which they called The Grove of Enthronement. This grove was about a half of a kilometre from the town. It was to this grove the Ọba-makers used to take one who was going to be enthroned. There they would put the sacred leaves of enthronement on the head of the man who was to be enthroned.

After several kinds of sacrifices had been performed for him as an Ọba, then they would clothe him in the royal robe and after, they would put the ade or crown on his head.

This Grove of Enthronement was very very beautiful and clean. Many kinds of very beautiful flower trees which attracted people indeed were there as well. In this same Grove of Enthronement, there was a small house. The length of the house was about twenty metres, its breadth was about fifty metres while its height was up to forty metres. Its walls were gold while its roof was silver. And that was the reason the Ọba-makers called this house The House of Gold and Silver. This house had no windows at all but one door which was fastened with the key of gold.

It was in this House of Gold and Silver that the senior Ọba-maker used to keep or hang the clothes and other kinds of property which they took away from the body of the new Ọba without knowing where his property was.

After, they would give him the gold key of the house to keep it in his possession in the Aafin or palace. But they would warn the new Ọba seriously not to attempt to open the door or to enter that house. But they would not tell him the reason why he was forbidden to open the door. This means the house is forbidden for the Ọba to open or enter it.

On the other hand, if an Ọba died while still on the throne, the Ọba-makers would bury with his corpse all of his property which was kept in the House of Gold and Silver. But if the Ọba did not die while on the throne but he committed an offence which deserved to dethrone him, then having taken the royal property back from him, the Ọba-makers would return to him all his property which they hid in the House of Gold and Silver and then they would expel him from the town. That was how the custom of the Town of Women went.

Now, when the junior Ọba-makers had covered Pauper with a large cover cloth and that he could not see now, the senior Ọba-maker who brought him to the town from the wilderness, took his dirty rags, the hair which was scraped from his head and chin, his bow and quiver. She carried all into the House of Gold and Silver. She hung all on the racks which were on the walls.

Having done so, she fastened the door with the key of gold and then she took it out of the lock. Now, Pauper did not know who took his hair, rags, bow and the quiver and he did not know where they were.

When Pauper was enthroned after several kinds of sacrifices had been performed for him, then the ade or crown was put on his head and after, all the costly royal property was handed over to him.

But then the senior Ọba-maker pointed with her hand the House of Gold and Silver to Pauper and she told him: 'Look at that House of Gold and Silver which you are looking far from here. Do you see it?'

'Yes, I see it!' Pauper replied as he fastened his eyes on the house.

'Take this key of gold! We open the door of the house with it!' She stretched out the key to Pauper and he took it from her with happiness.

'But as from today, you must not even go near the house, and as from today, when you go to your Aafin, you must not come back to this Grove of Enthronement! It is entirely forbidden for

122

the Oba who is already enthroned to enter this grove again. Do you hear me?' the senior Oba-maker warned Pauper who was the Oba now, in earnestness.

'I abide with your warning! And I will never go against your order.' The Oba (Pauper) made the covenant in the hearing of the rest of the Oba-makers.

After the senior Oba-maker had sworn in Pauper, the new Oba, she announced loudly, she said: 'Kabiyesi (Your Majesty) the Oba of the Town of Women!' But then the multitude of women shouted greatly with one voice of joy: 'Kabiyesi, our Oba! Kabiyesi, our Oba! Let the crown keep long on head and let the shoes keep long on feet! Kabiyesi!'

These shouts of joy were so much that all the people of the neighbouring towns which surrounded the Town of Women heard the shouts of joy. Without hesitation, these people began to run to this town to see what was happening there. But before they arrived, the Oba-makers had already taken the Oba to the palace.

But as soon as the Oba sat in the royal seat, the people arrived like the flood of water. Then all of them began to dance in joy.

Now, the Oba (Pauper) sat on the throne with ease and in great joy. But he was surprised and fearful when he did not see even a single man among this crowd of women. However, he kept silent. He thought in his mind that 'how long it will be, the stammerer will pronounce out baba (father)'. He thought perhaps in a little time more, the men would show themselves up to him in the end.

In the evening of the second day that the Oba-makers had worn the ade for the Oba, the multitude of women of the town came to the Aafin. They and the senior Oba-maker (the feeble old woman) and the rest of the junior Oba-makers accompanied the Oba to the assembly ground on which the people used to gather together whenever the Oba was performing an important ceremony.

When the Oba sat in the pavilion which was lavishly decorated for him, then the senior Oba-maker who was also the Herald for the rest of the Oba-makers began to announce to the gathering, she said: 'You all old women, you all young women and you all ladies of this Town of Women! It is with happiness to tell all of you that I had found one man from the wilderness, and I had brought

123

him to the town!' The Herald continued her announcement, she said: 'The full name of the man is Pauper, the Father of Wretchedness! And it was poverty and wretchedness which drove him out of his father's town!' the Herald said.

But now having heard this, the crowd of women hummed loudly at a time – 'Hun-un-un!' in great joy as they fastened their eyes on Pauper, the new Ọba.

The Herald went further, she said: 'As all of you are aware that we had been longing for men and the Ọba for years, and that all of you know well that a town without men is an insignificant town and by that it is useless!' The Herald went on, she said: 'Hereby, we the Ọba-makers have already enthroned him and we have taken him to be our husband as well!'

But when the gathering of women heard this joyful announcement from the Herald, they shouted greatly in joy and in happiness, they clapped loudly as they were rocking here and there on the same spot that they stood.

And as the Herald paused just for a while, the minstrels began to flatter the Ọba: 'Haaa! Pauper! Our Ọba! But what do we take the Ọba to be? None! Haa, the Ọba, the ruler! The Ọba who wears the crown of money! Ọba, the ruler! Ọba who walks with the beaded walking stick! Ọba, the ruler!'

But as 'it is for one who rides the horse goes galloping and arrives galloping', so Pauper, who was the Ọba now, began mincing himself to left and right when the minstrels were flattering him. And his doing so was another cheerfulness which added a sort of merriment to his coronation.

'Today is the end of our suffering for men after these years! The end of our suffering has come!' the Herald announced cheerfully. 'For this, we must thank our Creator for providing us Pauper to succeed our men and our Ọba, all of whom had lost their lives when they went and fought the people of another town in order to save this our town!'

But when the Herald announced to the women like that and that she mentioned their men who had lost their lives in the battle, they hummed sorrowfully for a few minutes.

'But do you all accept Pauper as our Ọba and husband or not?'

124

But the gathering of women hastily stretched their hands up and shouted greatly: 'We accept him as our Ọba and husband!' The drummers beat their drums and showed their happiness too.

As soon as the drummers and minstrels kept quiet, then the Herald faced the Ọba and she explained to him that: 'Kabiyesi, our new Ọba, with humbleness, I explain to Your Highness that for having no men in our town, the people of the towns and villages which surround our town changed the name of this our town from Town of Glory to the Town of Women!'

The Herald continued, she said: 'And moreover, as soon as all of our men lost their lives in the battle, the two holy ladies who are called Peace and Joy left our town for another town in which there was no war, rebellion, poverty, brawls or confusion. Because Peace and Joy do not live in the house or town which is not peaceful and joyful!' The Herald made their Ọba understand what had befallen their town.

'But you, Pauper, even though you are alien to us, you must try to take care of all of us who have become your Olori (queens) as from today!'

The Herald began to warn the Ọba, she said: 'But! But! I warn you again with hot temper that as from today you are entirely forbidden to enter into the Grove of Enthronement and you are also banned from opening and entering the House of Gold and Silver which is in the Grove of Enthronement. In fact, I have given you the key of gold of the house!'

The Herald went further in her announcement to the gathering of women and the Ọba, she said: 'But soon or later, we shall have the deputy Ọba. And I am sure, Creator who had provided Pauper to us will provide another man to us again who will be the Ọtun Ọba or Deputy for our Ọba!'

But after the Herald had concluded her announcement on behalf of the rest of the Ọba-makers, she bowed low for the Ọba and then she shouted: 'Kabiyesi, our Ọba!' And then the crowd of women joined her immediately, they said: 'Kabiyesi, our Ọba!' The drummers also greeted the Ọba through their drums. And so the minstrels did not shut up their mouths but they flattered their Ọba for a few minutes.

125

Now, Pauper (Ọba) was certain that there was not a single man in this Town of Women. But he remembered Slanderer when the Herald, or the feeble old woman, mentioned the Ọtun Ọba. He preferred Slanderer to be his deputy even if he was wicked.

Pauper's (Ọba) belief was that if Slanderer was under him he would take no advantage of his evil behaviours against him. But up till now Pauper never knew where Slanderer and Brawler, his wife, were. Because he had never seen them or heard any information about them since the day his hired canoe sank in the river near Atẹpẹ town.

After the Herald had announced to the gathering of women about their new Ọba then, in return, the Ọba thanked her indeed. After, he addressed the gathering, he said: 'You all people of the Town of Women, I thank the whole of you for accepting a poor and wretched man like me as your Ọba. I thank you all indeed!'

The Ọba began to tell about himself to the multitude of women as soon as he had adjusted his voice to that of an Ọba. He said: 'You my people, it is worthy to tell you even if in brief about my manner of living in which I was before I became your Ọba today!'

The Ọba continued his life history, he said: 'I was born in Laketu town. My father is the Ọba of that town. But my poverty and wretchedness had begun since my childhood. As a matter of fact, I am a hard-working one. But the harder I work the more my poverty and wretchedness become worse. Anything that I may lay my hands upon always come to poverty and wretchedness for me in the end!

'But of course, the people are telling me always that my destiny is that of Poverty and Wretchedness.' The Ọba went further, he said: 'But I don't believe them. Although they are sure that my poverty and wretchedness are so powerful that they are beyond the knowledge of human begins!'

The Ọba went on, he said: 'But later, the people started to call me Pauper, the Father of Wretchedness, instead of my surname!' But when the crowd of women heard like this from their Ọba, they shouted at a time: 'Haa!' And when he told them that the name of his wife was Brawler and that she had no other work which she was doing more than to brawl both day and night,

126

they shouted again: 'Haa! Brawler or what? Haa, you are unfortunate indeed!'

When the Ọba told the gathering again that the name of the only close friend he had on earth was called Slanderer, the gathering shouted greedily and then they said: 'Haa, your bad luck is over-much. And your people who had changed your surname to Pauper, the Father of Wretchedness, were right and they were to be commended!'

It was like that Pauper who was now the Ọba of the Town of Women told his life history in brief to the crowd of women. But as soon as he had finished his address, the crowd of women scattered suddenly in great laughter. But as they were rushing back to their houses, it was so they were clapping and singing along loudly: 'We have known it! Pauper is the name of our Ọba! We have known it! Pauper is the name of our Ọba! We have known it!'

Immediately the Ọba had finished his address, the royal drummers and minstrels started their amusements as the Ọba-makers were leading the Ọba to his Aafin or palace.

Now, in the long run, Pauper became an Ọba in a faraway town. Although the Ifa oracle had foresaid so on the third day that he was born.

Now, Pauper, the Ọba, began to rule the women and he was eating and drinking as he wished. A few days later, he had such rest of mind that he became fat and his poverty and wretchedness had disappeared from his appearance immediately.

But as Brawler and Slanderer were among those passengers who were carried away by the tides the day Pauper's hired canoe broke into two and sank near Atẹpẹ town, when the tides carried them to the part of the river where the tides were weak, Slanderer, Brawler and the other passengers swam on to the bank of the river.

But then Slanderer and Brawler started to wander about, looking for Pauper. But after a few days, Brawler and Slanderer quarrelled, so this caused them to part. Slanderer went to the north while Brawler travelled to the southward and she was searching for her husband.

But when Slanderer had wandered for some months, he came to one village, and he was told there that Pauper had become the Ọba of the Town of Women. But then he asked the inhabitants of the village where was the Town of Women and they showed him the road of the Town of Women. But it took Slanderer four months before he came to the Town of Women.

Slanderer feared greatly when he entered the town and the multitude of women rushed out and embraced him. Then without hesitation, they took him to the Aafin.

The Ọba (Pauper) was extremely happy when he saw Slanderer, his only close friend on earth. They embraced each other and greeted each other in great joy. But after their warm greeting, the first word which they spoke to each other was that: 'What the Ifa had foretold has come to pass in the end!' The meaning of this was that the Ifa said in 'ẹsẹnt'aye' or the future life of Pauper that he would become an Ọba in his wandering. And so the Ifa foretold in Slanderer's 'ẹsẹnt'aye' that he would be installed the Ọtun Ọba in a faraway town.

Then the Olori or queens served Slanderer with food and drinks. But as he was eating the food, the Ọba asked him whether he saw Brawler. He replied that he saw her. He told the Ọba further that they parted with a quarrel. But now, the Ọba was certain that his brawling wife, Brawler, was still on earth. Because the overmuch enjoyment of ọbaship or kingship had forced him to forget that he, Brawler and Slanderer had been changed to immortals by the Ọba of Laketu town in the name of Creator, and it was that same day that Creator changed Peace and Joy to immortals as well.

'But, Slanderer, don't you see me now in this great dignity? Did I not tell you that there was nothing like destiny?' the Ọba reminded Slanderer of his disbelief in destiny.

'It is just so. I believe now that there is nothing which people called destiny! However, let Creator forgive us our idle talk!' Slanderer replied confusedly.

The following day, the Ọba, the junior Ọba-makers and the senior Ọba-maker (the feeble old woman), all were thankful to Creator for providing again one man more for them. After, they started to prepare to install Slanderer as the Ọtun Ọba. And the Ọba was pleased with this preparation. Because it was Slanderer who was in his mind from a long time to be his Deputy or Ọtun.

Then the third day that Slanderer arrived in the town, the junior Ọba-makers took him to bath. Having removed all his dirty rags away from his body, they scraped the hair of his head and chin. They scraped also the hair of his upper and lower lips.

After, they gave him a thorough bath. Then they covered him from head to feet with the large cover cloth. Now, as he could not see, the senior Ọba-maker collected his hair and the dirty rags. She went to the House of Gold and Silver, she hung all on the racks and then she locked the door of the sacred house.

Immediately, the junior Ọba-makers brought Slanderer into the Grove of Enthronement, the senior Ọba-maker joined them. Then they performed the ceremonial rituals for him. But being he was to be the Ọtun Ọba, the rituals were less important than those of the Ọba. After, the senior Ọba-maker pointed her hand to the House of Gold and Silver. She warned him seriously not go there. Then she and the junior Ọba-makers led Slanderer to his Aafin or palace. His Aafin was not so far from the Ọba's.

When it was time to go to the assembly ground, the junior Ọba-makers, the senior Ọba-maker, the Ọba, the royal drummers, the minstrels and the multitude of women followed the Ọtun Ọba (Slanderer) on to the ground. The senior Ọba-maker who was the Herald for the rest of the Ọba-makers, told him about the Town of Women and she showed him to the crowd of women.

After, Slanderer, who was now the Ọtun Ọba, told the people about himself in brief, he said: 'But it is proper to tell you a bit of my countless evil characters!' The Ọtun Ọba continued, he said: 'Once upon a time, I was the most cruel and merciless raider, murderer, traitor, tale-bearer, slothful, treacherous person, etc., etc. who was ever born in my town called Laketu!'

But when the crowd of women and the Ọba-makers heard a bit of their new Ọtun Ọba's evil characters, they were overwhelmed with fear. 'I used to convert the destiny of people from favourable to unfavourable!' But when the gathering of women heard this from their Ọtun Ọba again, they were not aware when they shouted greedily in one voice: 'Haa! Why? You are indeed strange! But you alone had been behaving all these your dreadful characters? Haa! This is too "hard" and overmuch "hard" as well!'

The Ọtun Ọba advanced in his biography, he said: 'You should not be surprised at all about my cruel characters! These are my predestinations! Thank you all!' It was thus the Ọtun Ọba (Slanderer) addressed the crowd of women without shame.

But then the gathering of women, the Ọba, and the Ọba-makers, the drummers and minstrels led the Ọtun Ọba back to his Aafin as they were still wondering about his evil characters.

It was not so long before the Deputy started to eat good food and drink different kinds of drinks as he wished. He became very fat and his belly swelled out like that of a pregnant woman who would deliver a baby either today or tomorrow.

When the Ọba and his Deputy or Ọtun were enjoying much in this Town of Women, in a short time, both of them had forgotten entirely that they were once just like 'the sheep which does not change its last year's wool'.

The joy was so great for the Ọba that he forgot that it was poverty and wretchedness which he chose from Creator when he was coming to earth. Even he did not remember Brawler, his brawling wife, any longer. He forgot the year Slanderer (now his Deputy) deceived him and then both of them cut down his unripe maize. And he forgot as well that he was once a wood-carver.

Slanderer also enjoyed himself so much that he forgot the days when sometimes he got food to eat and sometimes hungered about. He forgot as well the day of his wedding when Pauper (now the Ọba) entered his tawdry image of the evil spirit and then he punished him nearly to death, taking revenge on him for his maize. And after, he caused him to lose his bride, Ọmọlere.

It was like that Pauper and Slanderer continued to enjoy themselves in the Town of Women without remembering their past sufferings.

But one evening, after the Ọba and his Deputy ate and drank and they danced merrily with their Olori or queens, then as the

Ọba sat in his royal state in his dignity, and his Deputy sat very close to him and lounged, he told the Ọba in haughtiness, he said: 'Hun-un, Kabiyesi (Your Worship). But you are the Ọba who is the ruler of this town and likewise myself who is your Deputy, or not so?'

'It is just so!' the Ọba replied in arrogance.

'But has the senior Ọba-maker (the feeble old woman) not given you the gold key of the House of Gold and Silver which is in the Grove of Enthronement?' the Ọtun Ọba asked.

'O yes, it is so, she gave the key to me. Even this is the key!' the Ọba replied cheerfully, stretching the key up and showing it to his Ọtun. 'But the senior Ọba-maker had warned me seriously that I should not open the door of the house!' the Ọba feared.

'O yes, I know. The senior Ọba-maker warned me just the same!' The Ọtun continued, he said: 'But why is there a secret in this our Town of Women which the Ọba and his Deputy should not know about? When both of us have the authority on this town and also on everything therein?' the Ọtun interrogated the Ọba.

'Well, this matter of the secret is obscure to my eyes!' the Ọba replied in confusion.

'Well, this is entirely disgraceful to the Ọba and his Ọtun when there is a sort of secret in this Town of Women on which the senior Ọba-maker insists that we should not know! Kabiyesi, don't you see it so?' the Ọtun Ọba lamented in earnest. 'Ọba, the ruler of earth and the second to gods!' the Ọtun Ọba gnashed the teeth and then he continued to provocate the Ọba, he said: 'Whereas the gold key of the House of Gold and Silver is in your possession! But my suggestion is that early in the morning we should go into the Grove of Enthronement with the key. With the key, we would open the door of the house to see the sort of secret which is in it!' But at this stage, the Ọba nodded and this meant he agreed to the advice of his Ọtun.

Immediately they concluded their plan, the Ọba poured the hot drink into his wine glass and so did his Ọtun. Everyone threw his own into his mouth and having gargled it in his throat joyfully, he swallowed it.

131

But then the Ọba replied fluently to his Ọtun's advice. 'That is exactly what we should do early in the morning. But you should make haste to come and wake me, so that we may go there and return to our Aafin before the people wake from their sleep!' the Ọba said cheerfully.

'Haa, Kabiyesi, don't you know who you have as your Ọtun? But I the cunning man! I would get in touch with you before daybreak!' It was so the deputy and the Ọba planned to go and open the door of the House of Gold and Silver.

'All right, goodnight, the ruler of earth and the second to gods!' the Ọtun stood up, staggering back to his Aafin.

'Okay, be going gently. Goodnight!' After the Ọtun had staggered away, the Ọba too stood up and he staggered into his room. He fell on his bed heavily and was fast asleep at once, for 'a drunkard forgets poverty'. The Ọba and his Ọtun were intoxicated strongly by the hot drinks which they were drinking continuously and which caused them to plan against the senior Ọba-maker's warning.

But it was hardly early morning, when the Ọtun came and woke the Ọba. After the Ọba had dressed in the best of the royal robes, he took his royal white tassel. After each of them took a full glass of hot drink, the Ọba took the gold key, then they left the Aafin or palace for the Grove of Enthronement.

When they came to the house, they stood in front of the door. But then guilty conscience began to trouble the Ọba. His hands began to shake so much that he was unable to put the key into the lock to open the door.

'But why are you trembling? Are you not the Ọba? Please, give me the key!' the Ọtun shouted to Ọba and then he snatched the key from him.

'But my conscience is just telling me that it will be unfortunate for us if we open this door!' the Ọba, in trembling voice and body, whispered to his Ọtun. But he had not yet finished his word when his Deputy heedlessly put the key into the lock of the door. He turned the key to the left and after, he kicked the door forward, and it fell inside suddenly.

The roof of gold and walls of silver of this house brightened its interior, which was very lovely and attracted people. But when the Ọba and his Deputy walked in in arrogance and the Ọba saw on the racks his dirty rags, hair of his head and chin which was scraped from his head and chin the day that he was enthroned, and his bow and the quiver, all of a sudden, the hair returned to his head and to his chin while his beautiful royal robes and tassel disappeared from his body at once. But his usual dirty rags returned to his body instead while his bow and the quiver returned on to his left shoulder. More, he became as haggard as when he was not an Ọba. Now, the Ọba looked like a madman as before.

As soon as all these things had returned to the Ọba's body, it was so for his Deputy. Immediately he saw on the racks the dirty hair of his head, chin and his dirty rags, the whole of them returned to his body as soon as his royal robes disappeared from his body. And he was now lean nearly to the bones.

As these dreadful changes came upon the Ọba and his Ọtun, suddenly and when they wanted to shout in greed, a strange thick darkness came over them unexpectedly. They could not see even themselves at all. But all at a sudden, they found themselves in the same wilderness, at the foot of the very mahogany tree from which the feeble old woman (senior Ọba-maker) took Pauper to the Town of Women several years ago.

This means Pauper, the Father of Wretchedness, and Slanderer, had now returned to their former multifarious ordeals. But of course, 'the tortoise's shell is a house of poverty; even if the tortoise is taken to a wealthy town, it will still return to its house of poverty'. That was just so for Pauper and Slanderer. Although the Ifa had foretold that in a faraway town Pauper would become an Ọba but in the long run, his Deputy or Ọtun would dethrone him by his cunnings. This means the Ifa's prediction came to pass on him in the end. And so 'destiny has no remedy'.

But when both Pauper and Slanderer became conscious, at the foot of this mahogany tree, Pauper, having looked and looked at himself and seen clearly that he had returned to his former poverty and wretchedness, in great earnest, he shouted: 'Ho-o-o-ro-o-o! Ha-a-a! I come back to my usual poverty and wretchedness! Ha-a-a! Is it true that what is called destiny exists? Is it the destiny of poverty and wretchedness that I had chosen from Creator?' Pauper was confused greatly.

And when Slanderer too looked and looked all over his body and he saw plainly that he had returned to his former wickedness and hunger and sufferings, with the topmost of his voice he shouted terribly: 'Paga! Ha-a-a! With my cunning hand, I have caused what has brought me back to my former misery and mischief! Ye-e-e! Ha-a-a! Woe unto me!'

It was like that Pauper and Slanderer continued to lament in great earnest which could not be described when the senior Qba-maker (the feeble old woman) appeared suddenly at the foot of the second mahogany tree which was not far from the one at the foot of which they found themselves.

# 25

# THE SENIOR ỌBA-MAKER REJECTS PAUPER'S
# AND SLANDERER'S ORAL PETITION

'Haa! The senior Ọba-maker, please help us! Even if we have heedlessly fallen into your trap of warning! But we apologize for our disobedience! We beg you in the name of the priest! Please reinstate us to our former Ọbaship!' Pauper and Slanderer lamented in tears to the senior Ọba-maker immediately she appeared suddenly at the foot of the second mahogany tree.

'Haa! Never! Your request and apology are not accepted! Inasmuch as you have abused my warning!' the senior Ọba-maker continued her protest, she said: 'Because you have opened and entered the House of Gold and Silver which is indeed a snare for every Ọba of the Town of Women!'

But instead of accepting their apology, the senior Ọba-maker started to taunt them in a mixture of whimsies and proverbs and they too were replying to her in whimsies and proverbs thus:

SENIOR ỌBA-MAKER: Haa, there you are in the end? (she snarled)

SLANDERER: Hun-un-un! O pity!

PAUPER: Alas! Even more than pity!

SENIOR ỌBA-MAKER: Fretting precedes weeping,

SLANDERER: regret follows a misfortune,

SENIOR ỌBA-MAKER: all sages of the country assemble,

PAUPER: but find no prevention for misfortune.

SENIOR ỌBA-MAKER: Haa! Little by little and in the end over-enjoyment has caused you to fall into the trap of the law; after my serious warning –

PAUPER AND SLANDERER: Haa, the senior Ọba-maker, unless

you release us from the trap of law; we swear, we cannot be good citizens again!

SENIOR ǪBA-MAKER: Hoo, it is much alas!

SLANDERER: Hoo, overmuch alas!

SENIOR ǪBA-MAKER: But there are two kinds of destinies,

SLANDERER: one is female – tender-hearted, favourable,

PAUPER: but the other one is male – harsh, unfavourable.

SENIOR ǪBA-MAKER: But the destiny of somebody is female,

PAUPER: and that one will find things easy and easy,

SLANDERER: and that one will be bearing children upon children,

PAUPER: and that one will be having more and more fine dresses,

SLANDERER: and that one will be getting money more and more,

PAUPER: and that one will not be wearing dirty rags all days,

SLANDERER: and that one will not roam about in nude,

PAUPER: but his manner of living will continue to prosper,

SLANDERER: and his manner of living will be sweet and sweet like the honey.

SENIOR ǪBA-MAKER: But that one whose destiny is male – harsh?

SLANDERER: that one will never get money in hand,

PAUPER: and that one will never get fine clothes to wear but except dirty rags,

SLANDERER: and like that of the madman.

SENIOR ǪBA-MAKER: The mouth that will not stop talking – ?

PAUPER: and the lips that will not stop moving – ?

SLANDERER: and it brings trouble to the cheek.

SENIOR ǪBA-MAKER: Even if he had been the Ǫba of the Town of Women?

PAUPER: but in the end, his destiny will dethrone him,

SLANDERER: but then he will continue to live in his poverty and wretchedness.

SENIOR ǪBA-MAKER: The cock which has a comb on its head – ?

PAUPER: that one has no tailfeathers,

SLANDERER: and one which has tailfeathers,

PAUPER: but has no dew-claw.

SENIOR ǪBA-MAKER: The one which has a dew-claw – ?

SLANDERER: but cannot crow.

SENIOR ỌBA-MAKER: But the poverty and wretchedness are the house of tortoise – I think – ?

SLANDERER: and if tortoise is taken to the wealthy town,

PAUPER: but in the end, it will return to its house of poverty and wretchedness.

SENIOR ỌBA-MAKER: Tóò! Well then, 'He who admits his fault in time does not keep too long in kneeling down to beg'. So our indefinite reunion is in the dream, and perhaps our indefinite meeting is on the road. Goodbye!

It was like that the senior Ọba-maker (the feeble old woman) rejected Pauper's and Slanderer's oral petition in whimsies and proverbs. After, she vanished suddenly.

# 26

# PAUPER AND SLANDERER BEGIN TO FIGHT

But as soon as the feeble old woman, the senior Ọba-maker, had vanished suddenly, Pauper and Slanderer began to brawl hotly on each other in great anger. But as 'the excess of joy makes the frog break its thigh', that it was such excessive joy which had caused Pauper and Slanderer to return to their former miserable condition. Although their reign as an Ọba and Ọtun Ọba was just a transient one. This had been foretold in their 'ẹsẹnt'aye' by the Babalawo.

'Slanderer, it was you who have caused what has brought me back to my poverty and wretchedness. Because it was not my intention at all to go and open the forbidden House of Gold and Silver. Otherwise I would still be the Ọba of the Town of Women!' Pauper blamed Slanderer in great sulks.

'Hun-un-un, "difficult to cure like an hereditary disease". Hoo, Pauper, that means you believe that the destiny which you had chosen from Creator will not come to pass upon you or what? That means when you were installed the Ọba of the Town of Women, your poverty and wretchedness had left you? No! But you are still in them!' Slanderer replied to Pauper in anger.

'I say it again, "if there is nothing wrong the thighs of the cricket would not have been broken". If you this wicked Slanderer had not put me in this undeserved punishment, I would not have returned to my destiny of poverty and wretchedness!' Pauper frowned at Slanderer in great anger, as both of them sat beside each other, at the foot of the mahogany tree in that dreadful thick wilderness.

'Please, Pauper, just stop that. What has gone, has gone for ever. The Ọbaship (kingship) is already lost to you. That is just "when the needle falls down from a leper's hand, he cannot pick it up again". And that is just so for you. But all I am after now is about my hunger. I am badly hungry now for food!' Slanderer simply disdained and disregarded Pauper's deep grief.

'Haa, Slanderer, that means you remember hunger or food when you have caused my dethronement with your wicked cunnings?' Pauper shouted suddenly in great earnest to Slanderer as he was sulky.

'Hee, hay-ay, look, Pauper, "a protruding tooth is the problem of the mouth"! But I am just looking for what I will eat now!'

Slanderer shouted to Pauper like that in an insignificant voice. And he told him again that, 'I am hungry cannot be expressed just by whistling'. Pauper, I say it aloud to you – I am hungry badly for food!'

Pauper was so much annoyed this time that he pulled one arrow out of the quiver. Then he hastily set it on his bow and without mercy, he shot it at Slanderer's left side suddenly. But just as 'the stone which is thrown at the bird in anger misses it', so the arrow simply missed Slanderer's side.

But now Slanderer knew well that the Ọbaship which had fallen from Pauper was such a grief to him that he was ready to hurt him, then he too, stood up, he hastily picked up from the ground one heavy stone. In anger, he threw it at Pauper's forehead. But it was just the same, 'the white termites simply try but cannot chew the stone'. Yet, the stone simply missed Pauper's forehead as well.

'Hoo, but Slanderer, is that so you want to retaliate? You wicked rogue! You evil man who have put me in trouble! That your hunger will continue for forever! But as you are aware that I am a strong man who fights with cutlass! I shall torture you beyond your endurance!' Pauper frowned at Slanderer.

But as he rushed furiously against Slanderer just to grasp him and slap at his ear, Slanderer feared so much that he did not wait. But he started to run fiercely along in this wilderness as he was abusing Pauper continuously that: 'Your poverty and wretchedness will continue to punish you forever!'

But in haste, Pauper hung his bow and quiver on his left shoulder. Then he started to pursue Slanderer. And it was so he continued to pursue him in great anger till when he pursued him into a certain town called Agbẹ-o-gbin'yọ.

# 27

## PAUPER, BRAWLER AND SLANDERER
## IN AGBẸ-O-GBIN'YỌ TOWN

In the long run, Pauper overtook Slanderer as he was chasing him about in Agbẹ-o-gbin'yọ town (farmers do not plant salt). But as both of them were engrafted to each other strongly, the people of this big town saw them and they rushed to them. Then they rescued Slanderer from Pauper when he wanted to tear him into pieces, even if he, Slanderer, and Brawler had been changed to immortals in their Laketu town before they were expelled from there long ago.

The great fearful noises of their fight were still roaring. When Brawler overheard the noises, then she ran with her brawls to the scene of the fight, just to see what was happening. But she was much surprised when she saw that it was her husband and Slanderer who were fighting. Then, in haste, she ran into the circle of the fighters. She held her husband. But when Pauper looked at the face of who held him, he saw that it was Brawler, his wife.

'Haa, are you this, Brawler, since when my hired canoe broke and sank into the river near Atẹpẹ town and then you were carried away by the tides with the other passengers?' Pauper was overwhelmed with astonishment.

'It is just so, I Brawler am this! But I had arrived in this town many years ago! Even I thought you have been wandering and got lost!' Brawler squabbled for many minutes.

'Never, I have not got lost!' Pauper replied.

'But where were you for these long years since I saw you last?'

'Haa, I was the Ọba of the Town of Women. But Slanderer,

141

with his wicked cunnings, caused my dethronement. But then I have returned to my usual poverty and wretchedness!' In grief, Pauper explained bitterly to Brawler as the crowd of people fastened their eyes at them.

'Paga! What the Ifa had aforesaid had come to pass upon you! But could you remember now that in the days gone by, the Ifa said in your 'ęsęnt'aye' that in your wandering you would become an Ọba in a foreign land, even though you were an alien there?' Brawler continued to remind her husband of the Ifa's forecast about his destiny. She said: 'But the Ifa said that in the long run, you would leave the throne but you would return to your destiny which is poverty and wretchedness!'

Brawler went further, she said: 'But I want you to be very certain as from today that "there is no bypath or short cut on top of the palm tree!" But indeed, you can never flee away from your destiny which you had chosen from Creator!'

After Brawler had reminded and warned her husband like that, she took Slanderer and Pauper to the Mansion of Sojourners in which she was living in this town. But after Brawler had roamed about, looking for her husband, and when she could not find him she travelled to this town. Then she started to live there. But at last, luckily, her husband came there and she saw him.

When Brawler took Pauper and Slanderer to the Mansion of Sojourners, she settled the fight between them for them and thus their fight was ended.

The Mansion of Sojourners in which Brawler was living was very big and it contained more than three hundred people. It had very wide premises as well.

The Ọba of Agbę-o-gbin'yọ town built this mansion for those who were sojourning in his town. When Brawler came into this mansion, the number of sojourners who were living there were more than three hundred. But as soon as Brawler came in the whole of them quitted the mansion in annoyance when her hurtful brawls were disturbing them from sleep in the daytime and night.

But after these people quitted the Mansion of Sojourners,

Brawler did not bother but she alone continued to live there.

Brawler and her husband, Pauper, however, were living in the same big room, while Slanderer, the cunning and wicked man, was living in another room which was at the far end of the premises of this mansion. Brawler and Pauper were so far from Slanderer's room that they could not know or see whatever he might be doing in his room. But sometimes, Slanderer was overhearing Brawler's hot brawls.

The following morning after Pauper and Slanderer arrived in this town, as Pauper had no money to buy the carving tools, the first thing that he did was that he borrowed some tools from his fellow wood-carvers who were in the town.

After, he went into the forest, he felled one big tree. Then he carved it into different kinds of images of masquerades and many other kinds of domestic utensils.

It was those things which he was selling for money. He and his wife were spending the money for their food.

But soon, Slanderer's cunnings helped him so much that he got the opportunity to get in touch with the Ọba and his chiefs. So, the Ọba appointed him his state Ikọ or messenger. The Ọba and his chiefs were sending him everywhere in the town to deliver messages. The Ọba and his chiefs were paying him a little money and remuneration like useless clothes as rewards for his work.

But although Slanderer was so greedy, since the day he had got a job from the Ọba and was then getting the remnants of food which were left in the Aafin, he ceased to come to Pauper. But Pauper did not bother whether he shunned him and his wife. Instead, he paid much heed to his carving work.

In fact, it was a bit difficult for Pauper to sell his carvings as he wished. Because each market day that his wife carried the beautiful carvings to the market, having set them on the ground for sale she then sat near them. But when those who wanted to buy them came and started to ask for the price of each, instead of telling them the prices, it was at that very moment she would start to brawl hotly like the dead.

But when the people waited for many minutes without her

143

telling them the prices, then in anger, they would leave her and go away. For this reason she would not sell even a single one of the carvings. But then she would carry them back to the house as she carried them to the market.

But the market day that her husband carried them to the same market for himself, those who wished to buy the carvings would not attempt to stop and ask for the prices of the carvings at all. But they would go on their way as hastily as possible. Because they took him to be a dangerous madman in respect of the dirty rags which he wore. And in the end he too would carry his carvings back to the house.

That was how Pauper's beautiful carvings were unsaleable in the market, except the few ones which he was selling in the town.

But because Slanderer was now one of the Ọba's Ikọ, he had so much advantage that one day, he stole the Ọba's crown, his beaded walking stick, his beaded shoes, his coral-beads, his Staff of Order and much royal property. Slanderer carried all into his room.

Slanderer did not stop at that. But in the night of the same day, he stole one of Ọba's Olori or queens. He hid her in his room as well. But Pauper and Brawler were innocent of all this deed of Slanderer's. Because he had boycotted them for a long time. But he used to hear Brawler's brawls in his far room which was quite out of view of Pauper and Brawler.

Even if Pauper and Brawler were just 'the sheep which does not change its last year's wool', they were living in their poverty, wretchedness, fight and brawls in righteousness and with contentment.

It was the third day that Slanderer had stolen the Ọba's property when the Ọba just observed that one of his Olori was missing from the Aafin or palace. But as soon as the Ọba had observed this, he sent for his chiefs. Without hesitation, the whole of them started to search for this missing Olori.

But it was when they were searching for the Olori when they saw that the crown, the beaded walking stick, the Staff of Order, the beaded shoes and the coral-beads of the Ọba were

144

also missing from the place in which they used to keep them in the Aafin.

Of all these missing property, the Ọba's crown and the Staff of Order were the most important ones which troubled the Ọba and his chiefs indeed.

The Ọba could not sleep and he could not nap. He could not stand still and could not sit down with ease and it was so for his chiefs. Food? No! Drink? No! There was none of them who could eat and drink. Because 'a disease that affects the Ọba also affects his chiefs'. What befalls the Ọba also befalls his chiefs.

Because even if the Ọba's crown was important, the Ọba's Staff of Order was also important for the Ọba and his chiefs. Because it is only with this Staff of Order the Ọba's Ikọ can arrest the offenders. And it is this same Staff of Order the Ikọ takes to one who the Ọba and chiefs want to come to the Aafin. When the Ikọ gives this Staff of Order to someone, he must follow the Ikọ with it to the Aafin immediately or if not, he has committed an offence. The Staff of Order is just like a summons paper.

At last, when the Ọba and his chiefs tried their best to find the missing property but failed to find it, they consulted one powerful Babalawo, the Ifa priest. They asked him to help them find out from the Ifa about the missing property.

When the Babalawo cast his Ọpẹlẹ, the Ifa's messenger, on the ground, then having studied the 'odu' which appeared carefully, the Babalawo interpreted it to the Ọba and his chiefs that the Ifa said that the Ọba's stolen property would be found in one of the sojourners' rooms.

Having heard what the Ifa prophesied, the Ọba and his chiefs were now happy and their minds were at rest. But as the Ọba and his chiefs were unable to hesitate till when the prediction of the Ifa came to pass, the Ọba instructed his Bell-ringer to announce round the town with the bell, to tell all the young men and old men and also all the sojourners to gather together in front of the Aafin the following morning.

But this Ọba's and the chiefs' emergency invitation was very fearful to the people of the town. For this, it was hardly morning when the people hastily set aside what they were doing, but they ran to the front of the Aafin. They sat down and were expecting what the Ọba and chiefs were going to tell them, whether good or bad they never knew.

It was not so long before the Ọba and his chiefs walked from the Aafin to the outside. Then the crowd of people hastily prostrated and they were greeting loudly: 'Kabiyesi, the ruler of earth and second to gods!' But then the Ọba shook his white tassel to them while his Herald, on his behalf, replied loudly: 'The Ọba greets you!'

But it was greatly strange to the crowd of people to see that there was no crown on Ọba's head and there were no beaded shoes on his feet this morning, whereas the Ọba had never come out to the crowd of people as this before without wearing his royal dresses. More, the people were also shocked when they did not see the sign of happiness on the Ọba's and his chiefs' faces as was usually so.

But as it is 'if there is no happiness in the house, the house will be just like the bush', is that the people never knew all that had happened in the Aafin.

As soon as the Herald (the Ọtun Ọba, Chief Ogundabede) greeted the people on behalf of the Ọba and chiefs, he announced to the people, he said: 'It is a few days ago since we have started to search for the Ọba's crown, his beaded walking stick, his coral-beads, his Staff of Order, his beaded shoes and also one of the Olori (queens)!'

The Ọba's Ọtun or the Herald continued his announcement, he said: 'We appeal to you all the people of the town and to you all the sojourners, that those of you who know one who had stolen the Ọba property, should please tell us!'

But as the Ọtun or the Herald had just concluded his announcement like that, it was at that moment Pauper and Brawler, his wife, who were among the sojourners in this Agbẹ-o-gbin'yọ town arrived.

As Brawler continued to brawl loudly in amidst the crowd of people and they were laughing loudly at her strange brawls, one of the chiefs remembered just this very time that it was in the

Mansion of Sojourners Pauper, Brawler and Slanderer were living together, and that Slanderer, being one of the Ikọ, was not among his fellow Ikọ who were in the gathering that morning.

'But what has caused Slanderer to absent himself from his duty this morning?' When that chief asked like that in suspicion, then another one of the chiefs said: 'But let us go and search that Mansion of Sojourners, perhaps we may find the Ọba's missing property there!'

But when this chief brought this advice, the crowd of people agreed to go and search the mansion at once. But then the people, chiefs and the Ọba and many of the sojourners pushed Pauper and Brawler in front of them. They followed them to the Mansion of Sojourners in which Pauper, Brawler and Slanderer were living.

When the chiefs, the Ọba and some of the boys entered the mansion, the first room which they searched was that of Pauper and his wife. But the Ọba's property was not found in it. After, they searched several other rooms yet they did not see the Ọba's property in them.

It was like that they searched one room and the other without seeing anything there until when they came to the room in which Slanderer lived, at the far end of the premises.

When they opened the door of his room suddenly, they met him inside the room, with the Ọba's coral-beads on his neck, the Ọba's beaded shoes on his feet, the Ọba's crown on his head. Too, they met the Olori in his room.

'Haa, Slanderer! You did all these!' the chiefs and the Ọba shouted in shock. But as it is 'the heavy rain which calms the birds in the bush', it was just so for Slanderer that morning. He was terribly afraid, he sighed and he became confused and haggard at once.

Without hesitation, the chiefs took the crown away from his head, the beaded shoes were pulled off his feet. They took the coral-beads from his neck. They took the beaded walking stick and the Staff of Order from him. After, they pushed him and the Ọba's Olori roughly to the outside. And just in the same

147

way they pushed Pauper and Brawler to the outside roughly although both were not offenders.

But now, Slanderer did not know what to say more than 'Haaa! Haa! Haa!' as they were pushing him, Pauper, Brawler and the Olori along to the Aafin.

Then the chiefs pushed Slanderer, Pauper and Brawler into the custody of prison for three days without giving them food or water. It was like that Slanderer put Pauper and Brawler in undeserved punishment. Although Slanderer was a habitual cunning man and the most evil-doer as well, all these could not help him this day.

But it was the third morning that the chiefs brought the three of them out from the custody of prison to the Aafin to judge their case and then to sentence to a long term of imprisonment one who was found guilty of the offence.

When Pauper, Brawler and Slanderer were brought out from the custody of the prison, they took them direct to the royal court of law, in the Aafin. It was Pauper who was asked to defend himself first. But he told the chiefs who were the judges that he was innocent of the Ọba's stolen property. After, the next person who was asked to give her own statement of the case was Brawler.

But instead of telling the court whether she knew about the stolen property, Brawler started to brawl continuously in front of the judges, the chiefs and the Ọba. But the chiefs did not understand all that she was saying in her brawls and also all were strange to the ears of the Ọba and his Deputy, the Chief Ogundabede.

But when the chiefs and the Ọba were tired of Brawler's useless brawls, they started to struggle to quiet her, but it took them more than ten minutes before they succeeded in stopping her from brawling.

But when it was Slanderer's turn to give his own statement, for him, it is just like 'the danger is in the farm of "Longe" and "Longe" himself is the danger'. While he was in the custody of the prison, he had already planned how he would defend himself before the judges.

And without hesitation, he pointed his hand to the Ọtun Ọba, the Chief Ogundabede. He told the rest of the chiefs and the Ọba that the Deputy Ọba was the right person who brought and hid in his room the Ọba's property which were the crown, beaded walking stick, beaded shoes, the Olori and the royal Staff of Order. Thus Slanderer, who possessed the whole evil characters of the earth, told a lie against the Ọtun Ọba.

'Haa! But Chief Ogundabede, you as the Ọtun Ọba, have done all this havoc?' the Ọba and the chiefs were shocked and shouted in one voice on Chief Ogundabede in uncontrolled anger.

'But I or who?' the Ọtun beat his breast in earnest as his eyes flashed out real fire at that moment. 'That means you all believe the lie which Slanderer has told against me to be true or how?' the Ọtun Ọba asked boldly.

'Surely and without even any doubt, all of us believe the allegation which Slanderer has made against you! Slanderer is not brave and bold enough to steal the Ọba's property!' the Ọba and the rest of the chiefs made disgraceful noises against Chief Ogundabede.

But now the Ifa's prediction on the Ọba's property that they would find them came to pass in the end, even if it was Slanderer who, as one of the sojourners, stole those things.

As I said earlier, the title of the Chief Ogundabede, the Ọtun Ọba, was the highest of all the rest of the chiefs. For this, he had much power in the town. He was tall, stout and was very strong. He was open-handed, kind and cheerful. So all this caused the children and young people of the town to love him much.

But what caused his father to name him as Ogundabede when he was born was that he came to the earth through the 'odu' ogundabede. So for this reason, his father simply named him after this 'odu'.

Certainly, this name is indeed frightful to people. Because the 'odu' ogundabede is mainly causing enemies and sorts of difficulties for one who is created for it and it also relates to stealing. But in the end that unfortunate person who possesses this 'odu' will, however, overcome his enemies, difficulties, etc.

149

But as the 'odu' ogundabede through which Chief Ogundabede came to the earth relates to stealing, therefore, he was pilfering when he was a youth but he had stopped doing so before he became the Ọtun Ọba, especially as soon as his father had offered the right sacrifice to the Ifa.

But then the chiefs and the Ọba began to clap loudly and disdainfully on Chief Ogundabede as a dishonest Ọtun Ọba. And again they began to sing the song of disdain in high tone, saying:

Ogundabede, the thief-o-thief! He stole Ọba's crown!
  -O-thief! Thief!
Ogundabede, the thief-o-thief! He stole Ọba's coral-beads!
  -O-thief! Thief!
Ogundabede, the thief-o-thief! He stole Ọba's beaded shoes!
  -O-thief! Thief!
Ogundabede, the thief-o-thief! He stole Ọba's Staff of Order!
  -O-thief! Thief!
Ogundabede, the thief-o-thief! He stole Ọba's Olori!
  -O-thief! Thief!

It was like that the Ọba and the chiefs stood up, clapping and singing tumultuously on Chief Ogundabede, the Deputy Ọba.

After a while, this hostile action turned to a great scuffle suddenly. But when the Deputy started to beat the rest of the chiefs and the Ọba mercilessly and they too were beating him in return, they kicked the Ọba unaware. Then the Ọba lurched and he fainted immediately because his backbone broke into two. But as the Chief Ogundabede, the Ọtun Ọba, was stronger than any of the rest, he beat them so mercilessly that every one of them was severely bruised.

But when the crowd of people who were in front of the Aafin or palace saw that there was a scuffle in the Aafin, and as they knew well that 'it is forbidden to throw the "Oluwo" upon the ground', and that also 'it is forbidden to flog the "Apena" with the whip', and as the people were certain that 'it is entirely forbidden for the Ọba of the town to wrestle with his chiefs', then, having seen all these unusual incidents, the whole of them scattered suddenly in fear. This matter became now 'if you cannot run, leave the way

150

for me'. The people disappeared at the same time, and soon the town was in disorder.

Just as the scuffle was going on in the Aafin and in the town, Slanderer who was the accused person and who caused this chaos, with his usual wicked cunnings, bolted away from the Aafin. He ran back to his room in the Mansion of Sojourners. Without hesitation, he started to pack his belongings and then to escape from the town.

But when Pauper and Brawler saw that Slanderer who was the offender but he put his offence on Chief Ogundabede, was preparing to escape for his life, they too bolted away from the Aafin and they ran back to their room in the same Mansion of Sojourners.

# 28

# PAUPER, THE FATHER OF WRETCHEDNESS, BRAWLER AND SLANDERER VANISH

Slanderer was packing his belongings together as hastily as possible and then planning to leave the town immediately. But Brawler put her own and her husband's belongings on her head, and 'in a wink of monkey', Pauper and Brawler left their room for the outside. Then they ran away from Agbẹ-o-gbin'yọ town. But it was not so long before Slanderer too put the bundle of his clothes on head and he followed them. But he could not overtake them till when the couple ran to one crossroads. Several confusing feeder-roads met at this crossroads.

But without stopping their feet there, Pauper and Brawler took one of these feeder-roads which was at the left. Then they continued their journey on it.

But when Slanderer chased them to these crossroads unexpectedly, and he stopped there. Because he did not know the exact one of the roads which Pauper and Brawler took.

As he stood at the centre of the crossroads in confusion and annoyance, he began to shout: 'This or that!' Thus he was pointing a hand to each of the roads. He wanted to know which one of the roads Pauper and Brawler took so that he might take it and continue to chase them along, because he was not willing to part with them.

But as this confusing crossroads confused Slanderer much, after a while he began to strike his chest with his hand and was talking aloud to himself in earnest: 'Haa, I, Slanderer myself? I, the man of men who is favoured by Creator with the whole evil characters of this earth! I, who have the art with which I put the houses of people into disorder! I myself who cause confusions in the ways of people! I, who put also the Ọba and his chiefs in chaos! But I, Slanderer, who have put Pauper's destiny in disorder. I who have changed Brawler's prediction into hot brawls!'

Slanderer went on, he said: 'I, for that matter! I am not in the same rank with Pauper and while I am not the same companion with Brawler! Haa! But "the land will be barren instead of dying!" All right! But if I can overtake Pauper and Brawler on the road today, I will torture them severely!'

But as Slanderer, in great earnest and anger was boasting loudly like that, he took the road which was on the right and then he went away. He thought that was the right road which Pauper and Brawler took.

It was like that Slanderer put the Ọba and chiefs and the people of Agbẹ-o-gbin'yọ (farmers do not plant salt) town in great scuffles, chaos and in confusions.

But as Pauper and his wife, Brawler, were travelling along on that road, Pauper confessed heartily now to his wife that he just admitted that destiny existed and that it was the poverty and wretchedness he had chosen from Creator when he was coming to earth. So Pauper said sorrowfully to his wife.

It was not so long before the two of them arrived at the area where the sky and land met each other, which is called the horizon. But here Creator called the Land of Judgment. And it was on this Land of Judgment that Pauper and Brawler met Peace and Joy. But it was not so long before Slanderer arrived and met all of them there.

It was on this Land of Judgment that Pauper, the Father of Wretchedness, Brawler, Slanderer, Peace and Joy stood for precisely seven days. Because there was no more road on which to continue their journey further. But of course Peace and Joy kept themselves a bit away from Pauper, Brawler and Slanderer. They did so because they never go near where there is poverty, brawls, slander, rebellion or where there is no peace and joy.

'But is Creator so cruel to certain people to cause their lives to be as bitter as bitter leaf? And moreover He is so kind to cause the lives of certain other people to be as sweet as the honey?'

153

It was like that Pauper, Brawler and Slanderer, having shook their heads sorrowfully, asked from one another as they stood on the Land of Judgment. But this question was far more than their knowledge so that there was none of the three of them who was able to solve it.

They were still in confusion at this question when the Judge of Creator came unexpectedly. Without hesitation and without seeing him, he covered them, together with Peace and Joy, with a sort of strange darkness suddenly.

Then as soon as the Judge of Creator came, he started to tell Pauper, Brawler, Slanderer, Peace and Joy that Creator sent him to them to judge their cases according to their behaviours. But he told them that before he would judge their cases he would explain to them as Creator told him to do the question which Pauper, Brawler and Slanderer asked.

But then he explained the whole of it to them that: 'Creator said that it is true that I created certain people whose livings are as bitter as bitter leaf, which we can call poverty, wretchedness and hardships. But that I created certain other people whose livings are as sweet as the honey and which we can call riches and many other kinds of the earthly wealths!'

The Judge of Creator continued to explain the question, he said: 'All those riches and wealths which I, Creator, have granted to the wealthy or rich people on earth, those wealthy or rich people will not bring anything with them when they are returning to my residence. And so for the miserable people, they will not bring to my residence their poverty, wretchedness and hardships. But they will leave all behind them on earth!'

The Judge of Creator advanced in Creator's message to Pauper, Brawler, Slanderer, Peace and Joy, he said: 'But the wealths and riches which I have granted to the wealthy and rich people are extremely risky for them. And their wealths and riches are temptation and the trap of law which I Creator have given them.

'But it is only a bit of risk for the miserable people on earth.' The Judge of Creator went further, he said: 'Because I, Creator have bestowed the wealths and riches upon the wealthy and rich people but not for themselves alone. However it may be, they

154

must give to the miserable people their share out of their wealths and riches. But if they fail to do so, they fall into the temptation which I put before them and this will debar them from coming to my residence above, except the miserable people who endure the poverty, wretchedness and hardships without being despaired will come direct to me!

'On the other hand,' the Judge of Creator concluded Creator's message, he said: 'your question which you have asked from one another is beyond the knowledge of mankind on earth. Before, I, Creator, put the people in joy and peace which had no end. But later, the people ignored me. This is the cause of their sufferings. But those who do my wish, peace and joy will be living with them forever!'

It was so the Judge of Creator explained the question to Pauper, Brawler and Slanderer and also for Peace and Joy that morning.

But then according to the instruction that Creator gave to His Judge to give judgment to Pauper, Brawler, Slanderer, Peace and Joy according to the behaviour of each of them, the Judge of Creator first covered the whole of them with the strange darkness before he explained the question to them. After not so long, he covered Pauper and Brawler with a sort of strange smoke. But then all at a sudden, both of them changed to that strange smoke. Without hesitation the smoke scattered all over the earth. But this was not the end of Pauper and Brawler.

As soon as Pauper and Brawler, his wife, had changed to the smoke, a sort of strange, very powerful whirlwind started to blow with full force. Then it began to bend both small and big trees here and there so much that many of them fell down. Because of the force of this whirlwind, the cloud of dust and litter of dry leaves scattered in the sky. But then the thunder began to roar greatly and the lightning began to flash here and there in the sky like arrows.

It was in these terrible confusions that Slanderer changed to this whirlwind and then scattered to every part of the earth at once. But this was not the end of Slanderer.

But as Peace and Joy stood on the same spot on this Land of Judgment, with the peace and joy that which could not be described, the Judge of Creator blew a sort of peaceful and joyful air on to them and then both of them changed to that air suddenly in peace and joy. Then the air blew away all over the earth at once.

But to these days, in the house or town in which there is poverty and wretchedness, brawls will be there, and in the house or town in which there are brawls, poverty and wretchedness will be there. Therefore, there will be no happiness.

Just the same, in the town to which the whirlwind of Slanderer blows, there will be confusions, scuffles, raiders, traitors, wars, rebellions, etc., etc.

Furthermore, in the house or town in which there is peace, joy, happiness, etc., that means the air to which Peace and Joy had changed, blows into it. Because all evil things are enemies of Peace and Joy. For this, Peace and Joy are never in the place where there is poverty, brawls, fight, scuffles, confusions, wars, slander, etc.

But now, as Slanderer was just like 'the most senior masquerader who comes out last from the shrine to show himself to the people', so he made Pauper suffer severely on their journey. It was so he put all the towns which they reached into confusions, chaos, scuffles, etc.

'Haaa! Before we can find an elephant we will go into the forest, before we can find a buffalo we will go into the grassland and before we can find a bird like the egret it will be an unknown time. But before we can find such an evil man like Slanderer we will be where the dead go and do not return.'

But as the Ọba of Laketu town had cursed upon Pauper, Brawler and Slanderer in the name of Creator, the day that they were expelled from the town that 'only the going of the dragonflies is seen but not their return', although Pauper, Brawler and Slanderer did not return to their Laketu town, being as they had been changed to immortals, to these days they are still roaming about invisibly on earth and yet they continue to trouble the people.